MW00875469

The Book of DRAGONS

Tales and Legends from Many Lands

THE BOOK OF DRAGONS

TALES AND LEGENDS FROM MANY LANDS

Selected and Edited by
O. Muiriel Fuller

Illustrated by
Alexander Key

DOVER PUBLICATIONS, INC.
Mineola, New York

Published in Canada by General Publishing Company, Ltd., 895 Don Mills Road, 400-2 Park Centre, Toronto, Ontario M3C 1W3.

Published in the United Kingdom by David & Charles, Brunel House, Forde Close, Newton Abbot, Devon TQ12 4PU.

Bibliographical Note

This Dover edition, first published in 2001, is an unabridged republication of the text originally published in 1931 by Robert M. McBride & Company, New York, under the title *The Book of Dragons*. While the four color illustrations by Alexander Key have been omitted from this reprint, all of his black-and-white decorations have been included.

Library of Congress Cataloging-in-Publication Data

The book of dragons : tales and legends from many lands / selected and edited by O. Muiriel Fuller ; illustrated by Alexander Key.
p. cm.
Summary: A collection of stories, ballads, and legends about dragons from all corners of Europe, as well as China, Japan, and the Bahamas.
ISBN 0-486-41983-5 (pbk.)
1. Dragons—Juvenile fiction. 2. Children's stories. [1. Dragons—Fiction. 2. Fairy tales. 3. Short stories.] I. Fuller, O. Muiriel, b. 1901. II. Key, Alexander, 1904– ill.

PZ8 .B6435 2001
[Fic]—dc21

2001047373

Manufactured in the United States of America
Dover Publications, Inc., 31 East 2nd Street, Mineola, N.Y. 11501

TO

RENÉE B. STERN

AUTHOR, EDITOR AND FRIEND

CONTENTS

The Story of Siegfried

BY MAUD MENEFEE

LONG, long ago, before the sun learned to shine so brightly, people believed very strange things. Why, even the wisest thought storm clouds were war-maidens riding, and that a wonderful shining youth brought the springtime; and whenever sunlight streamed into the water they said to one another: "See, it is some of the shining gold, some of the magic Rhine-gold. Ah, if we should find the Rhine-gold we would be masters of the world—the whole world." And they would stretch out their arms and look away on every side. Even little children began looking for the hidden gold as they played, and they say that Odin, a god who lived in the very deepest blue of the sky, came down and lay in the grass to watch the place where he thought it was.

Now this gold was hidden in the very deepest

rocky gorge, and a dragon that everyone feared lay upon it night and day. Almost all the people in the world were wanting and seeking this gold; it really seemed sometimes that they were forgetting every thing else, even the sweet message and the deed they had brought the world. Some of them went about dreaming and thinking of all the ways there were of finding it. But they seldom did anything of all they thought, so they were called the Mist-men. And there were others, who worked always, digging in the darkest caverns of the mountains, and lived underground and almost forgot the real light, watching for the glow of the gold. These were called the Earth-dwarfs, for they grew very small and black living away from the light. But there were a great many blessed ones who lived quite free and glad in the world, loving and serving one another and not thinking very much of the gold.

There was a boy whose name was Siegfried, and though he lived with an Earth-dwarf in the deep forest, he knew nothing of the magic gold or the world. He had never seen a man, and he had not known his mother, even, though he often thought of her when he stood still at evening and the birds came home. There was one thing she had left him, and that was a broken sword. Mimi, the Earth-dwarf, strove night and day to mend it, thinking he might slay the dragon. But though he worked always, it was never done, for no one who feared anything in the world could weld it, because it was an immortal blade. It had a name and a soul.

Each evening when Siegfried thought of his sword he would come bounding down the mountains, blowing great horn-blasts. One night he came laughing and shouting, and leaped into the cave, driving a bear he had bridled, straight on the poor frightened Mimi. He ran round and round, and darted here and there, until Siegfried could go no more for laughing, and the bear broke from the rope and ran into the woods. When Siegfried turned he saw that the poor little dwarf was crouched trembling behind the anvil, and he stopped laughing, and looked at him.

"Why do you shake and cry and run?" he asked. The dwarf said nothing, but the fire began to glow strangely, and the sword shone.

"Do you not know what fear is?" cried the dwarf at last.

"No," said the boy, and he went over and took up the sword; and lo! the blade fell apart in his hand. They stood still and looked at each other. "Can a man fear and make swords?" asked the boy. The dwarf said nothing, but the forge fire flashed and sparkled, and the broken sword gleamed, in the strangest way.

The boy smiled, and gathering up the pieces he ground them to fine powder; and when he had done, he placed the precious dust in the forge and pulled at the great bellows, so that the fire glowed into such a shining that the whole cave was light.

But the dwarf grew blacker and smaller as he watched the boy. When he saw him pour the melted steel in the mold and lay it on the fire, and heard him singing at his work, he began to rage and cry; but Siegfried only laughed and went on singing. When he took out the bar and struck it into the water there was a great hissing, and the Mist-men stood there with Mimi, and they raged and cried together. But still Siegfried only laughed and sang as he pulled at his bellows or swung his hammers. At every blow he grew stronger and greater, and the sword bent and quivered like a living flame, until at last, with a joyful cry, he lifted it above his head with both his hands; it fell with a great blow, and behold! the anvil was severed, and lay apart before him.

The joy in Siegfried's heart grew into the most wonderful peace, and the forge light seemed to grow into full day. The immortal sword was again in the world. But Mimi and the Mist-men were gone.

And the musician shows in wonderful music-pictures how Siegfried went out into the early morning, and how the light glittered on the trembling leaves and sifted through in little splashes. He stood still, listening to the stir of the leaves and the hum of the bees and the chirp of the birds. Two birds were singing as they built a nest, and he wondered what they said to one another. He cut a reed and tried to mock their words, but it was like nothing. He began to wish that he might speak to some one like himself, and he wondered about his mother; why had she left him? It seemed to him he was the one lone thing in the world. He lifted his silver horn and blew a sweet blast, but no friend came. He blew again and again, louder and clearer, until suddenly the leaves stirred to a great rustling, and the very earth seemed to tremble. He looked, and behold! he had waked the dragon that all men feared; and it was coming toward him, breathing fire and smoke. But Siegfried did not know what fear was; he only laughed and leaped over it, as he plunged; and when it reared to spring upon him, he drove the immortal blade straight into its heart.

Now when Siegfried plucked out his sword he smeared his finger with the blood, and it burned like fire, so that he put it in his mouth to ease the pain. Then suddenly the most strange thing happened: he understood all the hum and murmur of the woods; and lo! the bird on the very branch above was singing of his mother and of him, and of the gold that was his if he would give up his sword and would love and serve none in the world. And more, she sang on of one who slept upon a lonely mountain: a wall of fire burned around, that none could pass but he who knew no fear.

Siegfried listened to hear more, but the bird fluttered away before him. He saw it going, and he forgot the gold and the whole world, and followed it. It led him on and on, to a lonely mountain, where he saw light burning; and he climbed up and up; and always the light grew brighter. But when he was nearly at the top, and would have bounded on, he could not, for Odin stood there with his spear across the way. The fire glowed and flashed around them, but the sword gleamed brighter than anything that ever shone, as Siegfried cleft the mighty spear and leaped into the flame. And there at last, in the great shining, this Siegfried beheld a mortal like himself. He stood still in wonder. He saw the light glinting on armor, and he thought, "I have found a knight, a friend!" And he went over and took the helmet from the head. Long ruddy hair, like flame, fell down. Then he raised the shield, and behold in white glistening robes he saw the maid Brunhilde. And she was so beautiful! The light glowed into a great shining as he looked, and, hardly knowing, he leaned and kissed her, and she awoke.

And it seemed to Siegfried that he had found his mother and the whole world.

The Ballad of the Knight and the Dragon

RUMANIAN

HIGH up in the green forest of Cerna, at the borders of Serbia, there is a point where the Carpathian mountains seem to dip into the Danube only to emerge again on the other side and continue rising, forming the chain of the Balkan Mountains.

On the left bank of the Danube, at the ford of Rushava, lived three beautiful sisters, Ana, Maria and Rosana. Early one summer morning, before it was yet light, they stole out into the dew and mist. It was a holiday and they were to spend it singing and playing in the green woods they loved so well.

First came Ana, looking like a fair pink and white flower in her holiday robe. The second sister, Maria, was a vision of loveliness. Pride spoke in her walk and looked out from her big brown eyes which were bordered with thick, curling lashes. But the youngest sister, Rosana, was even fairer than the other two. Like a soft grey-blue dove she was, just flown from the nest. Nay, like unto both the evening and the morning star in beauty, surpassing even the radiant fairy Sanziana, and all Rumania knows how beautiful she is.

Not a care in the world had the three maidens as they played and frolicked in the wood. They gathered flowers which glistened still with diamond dewdrops, and wove them into wreaths for their hair and garlands for their robes. And while they twisted the flowers they sang the songs of their homeland, of their dear Rumania.

The forest echoed with their laughter and songs, and thus the day passed joyously, until the long shadows warned them day was nearly done. The youngest one, the fair Rosana, had grown weary ere this and had stopped to rest under a big tree, centuries old. Her two sisters had wandered on through the forest and now they turned their steps homeward without thinking of Rosana.

Still Rosana slept and twilight deepened into night. The birds hushed their singing and tucked their sleepy heads beneath their wings. The little stars came out and twinkled at each other, as if to say they knew the beautiful Rosana, fair enough to be a sister star, was sleeping in the forest. All night they watched over her until the first streaks of dawn chased them from the sky.

Then Rosana awoke and she was frightened at not finding herself safe in her white bed at home. She wept and called for her sisters, but there was none to hear save a little grey rabbit that scampered along a path in the forest. Yet there was another, a little cuckoo. Beautiful he was and brave. He flitted among the trees and sang with a loud voice.

"Dear cuckoo," called Rosana, "listen to me, you brave one! Lead me out into the open, to the road where carriages go by, so I can again find my home and my sisters. If you will do this, then I will be a cousin to thee!"

"Ah, my sweet one," sang the cuckoo. "I do not know whether I will lead thee into the open or not. I have as many cousins as there are flowers on the mountain and what should I do with another?"

"Cuckoo, cuckoo," implored Rosana, "listen, O brave one! Lead me out into the open, to the road of carriages, and I will be a sister to thee."

"No, my child, no," said the cuckoo. "I have as many sisters as flowers that bloom in the spring."

"Cuckoo, cuckoo," begged Rosana again, "listen, O brave one. Lead me into the open that I may find my sisters, and I will be a wife unto thee as long as I live."

"No, sweet maiden," sang the cuckoo, "that cannot be, for I am not a young man able to wed thee. I am only a little bird."

Even as the cuckoo spoke there suddenly appeared from behind a rock the horrible dragon of Cerna. Gruesome he was and cruel. He crawled across the path of the maiden and wound his tail around her. Rosana shrieked with terror, until the forest echoed with her piteous cries.

High up in the green forest of Cerna, where many brave men have lived and died, was a valiant

Rumanian knight, by name Ioan Iorgovan. His arms were like two great clubs, and he rode upon a horse that was as swift as an eagle. Two little dogs, quick and keen, followed his horse.

Ioan Iorgovan was riding gaily along enjoying the beauty of the morning. His horse pranced spiritedly and the knight waved his lance in the air, calling meanwhile to his dogs. Suddenly he heard someone crying. He stopped and listened but try as he would he could not determine what it was. Nor could he make out whether it was the voice of a man or woman. The mighty river Cerna roared loudly through the forest and drowned all sounds in its bosom.

So the knight turned back on the forest path and said to the river Cerna: "O my clean Cerna, stop, I pray thee, stop! I will throw into thy bed a silver lamprey and a golden distaff, with dragon's eyes, which will spin and turn by itself, if thou wilt but stand stiff."

The river Cerna heard him and at once stood still. Then Ioan Iorgovan, with arms like clubs, at once heard and knew the voice was not that of a man but of a woman in distress. Then he became angry and he spurred on his horse. Roaring like a lion and splitting the air with his cries, he came hurtling through the forest.

The dragon caught sight of Ioan Iorgovan racing toward him and he turned and ran away full of fear and trembling. But the knight was not to be put off. He followed hard after the dragon, until they both crossed the river Cerna. Then the dragon turned around and waited for the knight.

"Ioan Iorgovan, with arms like clubs," said the

dragon, "with what kind of a good message does thou come to me this day? Or hast thou the thought to destroy me? I pray thee, grant me peace and turn back to thy home. I swear if thou shalt kill me it shall be worse for the people of thy land. I will place a curse on the country and send a swarm of flies and they will bite the horses and oxen until the beasts will run mad and the plough will come to a standstill."

"O accursed one," cried Ioan Iorgovan, "dost thou still bandy words with me? I will teach the country and the people will hearken to me. They will raise smoke and the flies sent by thee will choke. My horse will not die but thou shalt perish, for I have heard thou hast killed a beautiful maid with thy robber's jaw."

"That is not true, Ioan Iorgovan," said the dragon. "When I heard thee coming through the forest roaring like a lion, I at once left the maid safe and unharmed. I pray thee, leave me alone and turn back to thy home. I swear on my head that it shall be worse for the country when I am dead."

But Ioan Iorgovan, with arms like clubs, was resolved to slay the dragon, for many were the tales told of the beast's evil doings in the countryside. So the knight seized his good sword and cut the dragon into pieces.

Rosana had been hiding behind one of the big trees in the forest where she saw everything that went on. She had recovered from her fright and approached the knight shyly and with maidenly dignity. Ioan Iorgovan thought she was the loveliest maid he had ever seen.

"Ioan Iorgovan, with arms like clubs," Rosana

said softly, "lead me out in the open to the carriage road, that I may meet my sisters, and I shall be a wife unto thee as long as I be alive."

Then wonder seized Ioan Iorgovan of her beauty and youth. He knelt at her feet and kissed her hand in reverence.

"My beautiful flower," said the knight, "thou art like a fairy. Thou shalt indeed be a wife to me as long as you be alive."

Then he embraced her and kissed her, and led her out into the open road where the carriages went by. The knight led the maiden back to her home and the wedding feast was celebrated right merrily.

But the blood of the dragon ran down into the river Cerna, until the water was red with it and it ran across the Danube itself. The curse the dragon had foretold came to pass, and a great plague of flies came upon the people of Rumania. The insects bit the horses and oxen until they ran mad and the plough was stopped. But Ioan Iorgovan, with arms like clubs, gathered the people together and taught them how to build fires and smoke out the flies until once more the country was at peace.

And today the people in far Rumania will show the imprint of the hoofs of Ioan Iorgovan's horse, and the footprints of his dogs on the high cliff overhanging the banks of the Danube.

The Dragon Sin

FRANCES JENKINS OLCOTT

ONCE upon a time, in ancient days, a fearful Dragon inhabited a certain forest. No one had the courage to subdue him, for his name was Sin. No knight, who ventured into the forest, was strong enough of himself to overcome the monster; and neither sword nor spear could harm him.

It chanced one day that the brave young warrior, Saint Leonard, was riding through the forest. He saw the Dragon Sin stretching out his hideous scaly length to prevent his passing by. Down from his horse the good Saint leaped, and crushed the monster in his arms.

Then backward and forward they struggled, the Dragon tearing Saint Leonard's flesh with his sharp claws. For three nights and three days, they wrestled thus together, then on the fourth day the Saint, breathing a prayer for help, drove the monster before him into the inner recesses of the forest.

And there the Dragon Sin stayed, skulking in the darkness; and he never ventured out again to attack the good young warrior.

Now as soon as Saint Leonard had conquered the Dragon, there was seen a wonder. Over the forest-ground were sprinkled drops of the Saint's blood, shed from his wounds. From them sprang up a host of Lilies-of-the-Valley, like a holy white carpet.

Then all the little Lilies softly chimed their scented bells in honor of Saint Leonard's victory for God.

The Green Dragon

COUNTESS D'AULNOY

ONCE upon a time there was a great queen who had twin daughters. Now it was the custom in those days to invite twelve fairies to come and see them and endow the babies with gifts. So the queen issued invitations and when the fairies had all assembled in the banquet chamber a magnificent dinner was served. They were just seating themselves at the table when the fairy Magotine entered the apartment. She was a wicked and malicious sprite and the queen shuddered at the sight of her, and feared some disaster as she had not invited her to the entertainment.

The queen carefully concealed her uneasiness and placed an arm-chair for the fairy, which was covered with green velvet embroidered with sapphires. As Magotine was the eldest of the fairies, all the rest made way for her to pass and whispered to each other: "Let us hasten, sister, to endow the little princesses, so that we may be beforehand with Magotine."

When the arm-chair was placed for Magotine she rudely said she would not have it, and that she was big enough to eat standing. But she made a mistake for the table was a high one and she was not tall enough even to see over it. This annoyance only increased her ill-humor.

"Madam," said the queen to Magotine, "I beg you will take your seat at the table."

"If you had wished me to do so," replied the fairy, "you would have sent an invitation to me, as you did to the others. But you would have only handsome persons at your court, with fine figures and fine dresses, like my sisters here. As for me, I am too ugly and too old. But for all that, I have no less power than they and without boasting of it, I may perhaps have more."

All the fairies pressed her so much to sit down to the table that at length she consented. A golden basket was placed before them containing twelve bouquets made of jewels. The fairies who had arrived first each took her bouquet, so that there was not one left for Magotine, who began to mutter between her teeth. The queen ran to her cabinet and brought out a casket of perfumed Spanish morocco, covered with rubies and filled with diamonds. She prayed Magotine to accept it, but the spiteful fairy shook her head and said to her: "Keep your jewels, madam. I have enough and to spare. I only came to see if you had thought of me. You have neglected me shamefully."

Thereupon she struck the table with her wand and all the dainties with which it was loaded turned into fricasseed serpents. The fairies were all so horrified that they flung down their napkins and left the table.

While they were talking together about the sad trick Magotine had played them, that cruel little fairy approached the cradle in which the princesses were lying wrapped in their swaddling clothes of cloth of gold, looking fresh and lovely.

"I endow thee," she said rapidly to one of them, "with perfect ugliness."

She was about to utter some malediction on the other baby princess when the fairies in great agitation ran and stopped her. On which the mischievous Magotine broke one of the window panes and darted through it like a flash of lightning, vanishing from their sight.

All the gifts which the good fairies could bestow on the princess could not console the queen. She took the baby in her arms and had the misery to see it grow more hideous every instant. She struggled in vain to suppress her tears in the presence of their fairy ladyships but she could not prevent weeping, and it is impossible to imagine the compassion they felt for her.

"What shall we do, sisters?" said they to each other. "What shall we do to console the queen?"

They held a grand council on the subject and finally told the queen not to give way to so much grief as there was a time coming when her daughter would be very happy.

"But will she become beautiful again?" asked the queen.

"We cannot give you any further information," replied the fairies. "Be satisfied, madam, with the assurance that your daughter will be happy."

The queen thanked them very much and loaded them with presents before they took their departure.

The queen named her eldest daughter Uglinette and the youngest La Belle. These names suited them perfectly, for Uglinette became so ugly that in spite of all her intelligence it was not possible to look at her, while her sister's beauty increased hourly and her appearance was altogether charming. The consequence was that when Uglinette was twelve years old she threw herself at the feet of the king and queen and implored them to permit her to go and shut herself up in a lonely castle far from the court, in order that she might afflict them no longer with her ugliness. As in spite of her hideous appearance they were fond of her, it was not without some pain they consented to let her depart. But La Belle remained with them and that consoled them.

Uglinette begged the queen to send nobody with her but her nurse and a few officers to wait on her. "You need not be under any fear, madam, of my being run away with," said she. "I can assure you that being what I am, I would willingly avoid even the light of day."

The king and queen granted her wish and she was conducted to the lonely castle. It had been built many ages ago, and the sea came in close under its windows. There was a large forest in the neighborhood, to walk or ride in, and several meadows stretched beyond it. The princess played upon the lute and sang divinely. She also wrote prose and poetry. She thus passed two years in agreeable solitude, but her desire to see the king and queen again induced her to visit the court.

Uglinette arrived just as they were about to celebrate the marriage of La Belle. The joy was universal, but the moment they beheld the poor ugly princess everybody looked distressed. She was neither embraced nor caressed by any of her relations and the only thing they had to say to her was that she had grown very much uglier. They advised her not to appear at the ball but said if she wished to see it they would manage to find some hole for her to peep through. She replied that she had come there neither to dance nor to hear the music but as she had been so long in the lonely castle she could not resist paying her respects to the king and the queen. She said further that she knew they could not endure the sight of her and that she would therefore return to her wilderness, where the trees, flowers and the fountains did not reproach her with her ugliness when she wandered among them.

When the king and queen saw she was so much hurt they told her with some reluctance that she might stay two or three days with them. But she was a girl of high feeling and she said it would give her more pain to leave them if she passed so much time in their good company. They were too anxious for her departure to press her to stay, and therefore coldly said she was quite right.

The Princess La Belle gave her an old ribbon which she had worn all winter in a bow on her muff, and the king La Belle was going to marry gave her some cotton taffeta with which to make a petticoat. Poor Uglinette would have willingly thrown the ribbon and taffeta in the faces of her relatives, but she had so much good sense and judgment that she exhibited no ill temper. So with her faithful nurse she left the court to return to her castle, her heart so full of grief that she never spoke a word on the whole journey.

One day as she was walking in one of the most gloomy avenues in the forest, she saw at the foot of a tree a large green dragon, which said to her: "Uglinette, thou art not the only unhappy creature. Look at my horrible form and know that I was born handsomer even than thou wert."

The princess was greatly terrified and heard not one-half of these words. She fled from the spot and for many days did not venture to leave the castle, so much was she afraid of meeting with the dragon again. One evening, weary of sitting alone in her room, she came down to the beach and walked along by the sea. She was pacing slowly to and fro, musing on her sad fate, when she saw sailing towards her a little boat, painted and gilded all over with a thousand various devices. The sail was of gold brocade, the mast of cedar, the oars of sandal-wood. It appeared to be drifting at random and it came close in to shore. The princess was curious to inspect all its beautiful decorations and stepped on board. She found it fitted up with crimson velvet on a gold ground, the nails being all diamonds.

Suddenly the boat was borne to sea again and the princess, alarmed at the impending danger, caught up the oars and endeavored to row back to the beach. Her efforts were in vain and the wind rose and the waves ran high. She lost sight of land and seeing nothing around her but sky and sea, resigned herself to her fate, fully assured that it was little likely to be a happy one and that it was another malicious trick of the fairy Magotine.

"I must die," she said, "but wherefore this secret dread of death? Alas, have I ever yet enjoyed any of those pleasures of life which might cause me to regret leaving it? My ugliness disgusts even my nearest relatives. My sister is a great queen and I am consigned to exile in the depths of a wilderness, where the only companion I have found is a dragon who can speak. Is it not better that I should perish than drag on so miserable an existence?"

With these reflections she dried up her tears and courageously looked out for the quarter from which death would come. Then over the billows, making its way towards the vessel, she saw the green dragon she had met in the forest. It approached the boat and said: "If you are willing to receive some assistance from a poor green dragon like me, I am able to save your life."

"Death is less frightful to me than thou art," exclaimed the princess. "And if thou seekest to do some kindness never let me set eyes on thee again."

The green dragon gave a long sigh and without answering a word went immediately under the water.

"What a horrible monster!" said the princess to herself. "He has green wings, a body of a thousand colors, ivory claws, fiery eyes, and on his head is a bristling mane of long hair. Oh, I would much rather die than owe my life to him! But what motive has he in following me, I wonder? And by what accident has he the power of speaking like a rational being?"

She was thus musing when a voice in answer to her thoughts said: "Learn, Uglinette, that the green dragon is not to be despised. Were it not a harsh thing to say to thee, I might assure thee he is less hideous in the sight of his species than thou art in the eyes of thine. But far from desiring to annoy thee our wish is to lighten thy sorrows, provided thou dost consent."

This voice greatly surprised the princess and the words it uttered appeared to her so unjustifiable that she could not suppress her tears. As she wept over her fate the vessel, which was completely at the mercy of the winds, drifted on till it struck upon a rock and went immediately to pieces. The poor princess caught at some pieces of the wreck and clung, as she imagined, to them. She felt herself supported in the water and happily reached the shore at the foot of a great rock. What was her horror when she discovered that her arms were clasping the wing of the green dragon! Seeing her terror the dragon drew back a short distance from her and said: "You would fear me less if you knew me better, but it is my hard fate to terrify all who see me." With that he plunged into the waves, and Uglinette remained alone upon the rock which towered high above her.

On whichever side she cast her eyes she saw nothing to save her from despair. Night was approaching and she was without food and knew not were to go. "I thought to perish in the ocean," she reflected sadly, "but here doubtless is the end reserved for me. Some sea monster will come and devour me, or I shall die of hunger."

She climbed up and seated herself on the summit of the rock. As long as it was light she gazed upon the ocean, and when it was quite dark she took off her taffeta petticoat and covered her head with it, remaining in trembling expectation of what might befall her. Sleep at length overpowered her and presently she thought she heard the music of several instruments. She thought she was dreaming, but a moment afterwards she heard someone sing the following verse which seemed to have been written expressly for her:

Do not shrink from Cupid's arrows,
Here his gentle sway we own;
Love with pleasure will surround thee,
In this isle no grief is known.

The attention she paid to these words had the effect of waking her completely. "What good or ill fortune now awaits me?" she exclaimed. "Can there yet be happy days in store for one in my wretched condition?"

She opened her eyes timidly, afraid of seeing herself surrounded by monsters. But what was her astonishment when in place of the rude and terrible rock she saw an apartment, the walls and ceiling of which were entirely of gold. She was lying in a bed which perfectly corresponded in its magnificence with the rest of this most splendid palace. She could not believe she was wide awake, and got up and walked over to a glass door which opened on to a wide balcony. She looked down upon gardens filled with flowers, fountains, statutes and the rarest trees. Woods stretched out in the distance, and she saw palaces of dazzling beauty, each one a masterpiece of architecture, with jeweled walls and roofs of pearls. Far to her right a calm and smiling sea gleamed in the sun, its surface covered with thousands of vessels whose white sails fluttered in the breeze.

"What do I see?" exlaimed the princess. "Where am I? What has become of the terrible rock that seemed to threaten the skies with its lofty pinnacles? Can I be she who was shipwrecked last night and saved by a dragon?"

She continued thus to talk to herself, walking about and stopping in perfect bewilderment. At length she heard a noise in the apartment and she reentered it. Advancing towards her were a hundred pagods, or figures with movable heads, formed and dressed in a hundred different fashions. The tallest were about a foot and a half in height and the shortest not above four inches. Some were beautiful, graceful and agreeable. Others were alarmingly ugly. Their bodies were of diamonds, emeralds, rubies, pearls, crystal, amber, coral, porcelain, gold, silver, brass, bronze, iron, wood and clay. Some were without arms, others without feet, while still others had mouths extending to their ears, eyes all askew and broken noses. In a word, there was as much variety among the pagods as among human beings.

Those who presented themselves before the princess were the deputies of the kingdom. After an oration, they entertained her by the information that for some time past they had traveled about the world but that in order to obtain their sovereign's permission to do so, they took an oath not to speak during their absence. Some there were indeed so scrupulous they would not even shake their heads or move their hands or feet, but that the majority of them could not help it. That in this way they traversed the universe, and when they returned they amused the king by telling him everything that had occurred in all the courts they visited.

"A pleasure, madam," added one of the deputies, "which we shall have the honor of occasionally affording you, for we are commanded to neglect nothing which can entertain you. In lieu of bringing you presents, we now come to amuse you with our songs and dances."

They began immediately to sing, dancing at the same time to the music of tambourines and castanets, while the princess watched and listened with delight. When they ceased dancing and singing, the deputy who had been spokesman said to the princess: "Here, madam, are a hundred pagodines, who have been selected to have the honor of waiting on you. Every wish you can have in the world will be gratified, provided you consent to remain among us."

The pagodines appeared in their turn, carrying baskets proportioned to their own size and filled with a hundred different articles which were so pretty, so useful, so well made and so costly that Uglinette was never weary of admiring and praising them. She uttered exclamations of wonder and delight at all the marvels they displayed to her. The most prominent pagodine, who was a little figure made of diamonds, suggested that she enter the grotto of the baths, as the heat of the day was increasing. The princess proceeded in the direction indicated, between two ranks of bodyguards whose forms and appearance were enough to make one die with laughter.

She found in the grotto two baths of crystal, ornamented with gold and full of scented water. The baths were under a pavilion of green and gold brocade. The princess inquired why there were two, and the pagods answered that one was for her and the other for the king of the pagods.

"But where is he, then?" asked the princess.

"Madam," they answered, "he is at present with the army, making war on his enemies. You will see him as soon as he returns."

The princess then inquired if he were married. They said no, that he was so charming no one had ever yet been found worthy of him. She indulged her curiosity no further, but undressed and entered the bath. All the pagods and pagodines began to sing and play on various instruments, and everything was so perfect and so well harmonized, that nothing could surpass the delight experienced at their concerts.

When the princess came out of her bath they presented her with a magnificent dressing-gown. Several pagods who played the flute and the hautboy marched before her and a train of pagodines followed her, singing songs in her praise. In this state she entered an apartment, where the pagodines in waiting and the pagodines of the bedchamber bustled about, dressed her hair, put on her robes, praised her and admired her. There was no longer talk of her ugliness, of cotton taffeta petticoats, or frayed muff ribbons.

The princess was truly astonished. "To whom can I be indebted for such extraordinary happiness?" she said to herself. "I was on the brink of destruction. I awaited death, and could hope for nothing else. Now I suddenly find myself in the most beautiful and magnificent place in the world, where I am received with the greatest joy."

As the princess was endowed with great good sense and good nature, she conducted herself in such a manner that all the little creatures who approached her were enchanted at her behavior.

Every morning, at her levee, she was presented with new dresses, new laces, new jewels. It was a great pity she was so ugly, but eventually she who could not abide herself began to fancy she was less disagreeable because of the great pains the pagodines took in attiring her. She scarcely passed an hour without some pagods coming to visit her, and telling her all the most curious and interesting things that happened in the world.

She occasionally saw some pagods who were large and fat and had such puffed out cheeks that they were wonderful to look at. When she asked them the cause they said: "As we are not permitted to laugh or to speak during our travels, and are constantly witnessing all sorts of absurdities and follies, our inclination to laugh is so great that the suppression of it swells up and causes what may properly be called risible dropsy, of which we cure ourselves as soon as we get home."

There was scarcely an evening without a performance of some play or a beautiful ball. The most diminutive pagods danced on the tight rope, in order to be better seen. Each banquet given for the princess was a splendid feast, and she enjoyed every minute of the day and night. They brought her books of every description—serious, amusing, historical. The days ran by swiftly, and the princess thought it was the most amusing thing in the world to hear the chattering of the little pagodines, whose voices were shriller than those of the puppets in a show at the fair.

It happened one night that the princess could not sleep, and she said to herself: "What is to become of me? Shall I always remain here? I pass my days more agreeably than I could have ventured to hope, yet something is wanting to my heart. I know not what it is, but I begin to feel that this round of pleasures, unvaried by a single event, is rather insipid."

"Ah, princess," said a voice, as if in answer to her thoughts, "is it not your own fault? If you would consent to love, you would soon know that it is possible to remain with a beloved object not only in a palace but in a wilderness for ages without wishing to leave it."

"What pagodine speaks to me?" inquired the princess. "What pernicious advice does she give me that threatens my future peace?"

"It is not a pagodine," replied the voice, "who forewarns you of what will sooner or later occur. It is the unhappy sovereign of this realm, who adores you, madam, and who cannot tell you so without trembling."

"A king who adores me!" replied the princess.

"Has that king eyes or is he blind? Can he know that I am the ugliest person in the world?"

"I have seen you, madam," answered the invisible king, "and have not found you what you represent yourself. Be it for your person, your merits or your misfortunes, I repeat, I adore you, but my respectful and timid affection obliges me to conceal myself."

"I am indebted to you for so doing," replied the princess, "but alas, what would be my fate should I love anyone?"

"You would give happiness to him who cannot live without you," said the voice, "but he will not venture to appear before you without your permission."

"No, no," said the princess, "I would avoid seeing any object that might too powerfully interest me." The voice was silent and the princess remained awake all the rest of the night in deep meditation on this adventure.

However she might have resolved not to say the least word to anyone about it, she could not resist asking the pagods if their king had returned. They said no, and this so ill agreed with what she had heard that it disturbed her. She continued her inquiries as to whether their king was young and handsome, and they told her that he was young, handsome and very amiable. She asked if they frequently received intelligence of him and they replied, "Every day."

But the princess still persisted. "Does he know that I am in his palace?" she asked.

"Yes, madam," answered her attendants, "he knows everything that occurs here concerning you.

He takes great interest in it and every hour a courier is sent off to him with an account of you."

The princess was silent and became much more thoughtful than she had formerly been. Whenever she was alone the voice spoke to her. Sometimes she was alarmed at it, but at other times she felt pleased, for nothing could be more polite than its language to her.

"Although I have resolved never to love," the princess said to the voice one evening, "and have every reason to defend my heart against an attachment which could only be fatal to it, I nevertheless confess to you that I should much like to behold a king who has so strange a taste. For if it be true that you love me, you are perhaps the only being in the world who could be guilty of such a weakness for a person so ugly as I am."

"Think of me whatever you please, adorable princess," replied the voice. "I find in your merit a sufficient justification for my passion. Nor is it from singularity of taste that I conceal myself. I have motives so melancholy that if you knew them you could not refrain from pitying me."

The princess then pressed the voice to explain itself, but it ceased to speak and she only heard long and heavy sighs. All these circumstances made her very uneasy. Although her lover was unknown and invisible to her, he paid her a thousand delicate attentions. Added to this, the beautiful place she was in induced her to desire society more suitable to it than that of the pagods. She consequently began to feel tired and dull everywhere. The voice of her invisible admirer alone had power to please her.

Waking suddenly one exceedingly dark night, she found that somebody was seated beside her bed. She thought it was the pagodine of pearls, who had more intelligence than the others and used sometimes to come and keep her company. The princess stretched out her arm to take hold of her but the person seized her hand, pressed it and kissed it, dropping some tears upon it, and was evidently too much affected to speak. She was convinced it was the invisible monarch.

"What would you of me?" she said to him, sighing. "Can I love you without knowing or seeing you?"

"Ah, madam," he replied, "by what conditions do you fetter the delight of obeying you? It is impossible for me to appear before you. The same wicked Magotine who has so ill-treated you has condemned me to suffer for seven years. Five have already passed. Two yet remain, the misery of which you could entirely relieve by accepting me for your husband. You will think me a rash fool and that I am asking an absolute impossibility, but if you knew, madam, the excess of my love for you and the extent of my misfortunes, you would not refuse me the favor I implore of you."

Uglinette found the invisible king everything that could be most charming in conversation and love took possession of her heart under the dangerous guise of pity. She replied that she must be allowed some days to consider it, for it was an important matter and she required time to think it over. The fêtes and the concerts recommenced with increased splendor. Presents were continually brought her, surpassing all that had been seen before. The enamored voice wooed her in the sweetest accents as soon as it was dark, and the princess retired at an earlier hour in order to have more time to listen to it.

At length she consented to marry the invisible king and gave him her promise that she would not attempt to see him until the full term of his penance had expired.

"It is of vital importance," the king said to her, "both to you and to me. Any imprudent curiosity you might indulge in would bring on me a renewal of my penance and involve you in a like misfortune. But if you can resist the evil counsels that will be given you, you will have the satisfaction of finding me all your heart desires and of regaining at the same time the marvelous beauty of which the malicious Magotine deprived you."

The princess was overjoyed at this new hope and vowed a thousand times to her husband that she would indulge in no curiosity without his permission. So the nuptials took place and the princess was married to her invisible lover.

After some time had passed Uglinette was desirous of seeing her family. She asked her husband if she might bring them to their kingdom and a vessel manned by pagods and laden with presents was sent with letters from Queen Uglinette to the queen her mother, asking her to come and pay a visit to her daughter in her own dominions. The pagods who were charged with this mission were permitted on this occasion only to speak.

The loss of the princess had not been entirely unfelt by her relatives. They believed she had perished and consequently her letter gave great delight to the court. The queen lost not a moment in setting out with her other daughter and her son-in-law. The pagods, who alone knew the way to their kingdom, safely conducted thither the whole royal family, and when Uglinette saw her family once more she was ready to die with joy. She was on her guard against questions about her husband, but she made a hundred mistakes. Sometimes she said the king was with the army; sometimes that he was ill, and in no mood to see anyone; sometimes that he was on a pilgrimage; and at others, hunting or fishing. At last it seemed as if she was pledged to talk nothing but nonsense and that the barbarous Magotine had unsettled her wits.

Her mother and sister consulted together on the subject and came to the conclusion that she was deceiving them and might probably be deceiving herself. They therefore with ill-directed zeal resolved to tell her so and managed very skilfully to infect her mind with a thousand doubts and fears. After having refused for a long time to acknowledge the justice of their suspicions, she at last confessed that up to that period she had never seen her husband, but that his conversation was so charming that it was sufficient happiness to listen to it. He had yet two years to pass in this state of penance, but that at the end of that time not only should she behold him but become herself beautiful as day.

"Oh, unfortunate creature!" exclaimed the queen. "How gross is the snare they have laid for thee! Is it possible that thou couldst have listened with such extreme simplicity to such fables? Thy husband is a monster. How could it be otherwise for all the pagods, of whom he is the king, are downright monkeys."

"I believe, rather," said Uglinette, "that he is the God of Love himself."

"What a delusion!" cried Queen La Belle. "You are positive that Cupid is your husband and to a certainty he is a monster. At least satisfy your mind on this point. Enlighten yourself on that matter, as you may do so easily."

The queen said as much and her son-in-law still more. The poor princess was so confused and so agitated that after having sent all her family home laden with presents, which fully repaid the cotton taffeta and the muff ribbon, she resolved come what would to obtain a sight of her husband. She concealed a lamp in her room and when her invisible husband visited her that night she turned the light full upon him. What shrieks she uttered when instead of beholding as she thought the tender Cupid, fair, white, young and in every way charming, she saw revealed the horrible green dragon with his long bristling mane. He was in a paroxysm of rage and despair.

"Cruel woman," he cried, "is this the reward of so much affection?" But the princess did not hear him. She fainted in terror and the dragon in an instant was far away.

At the disturbance caused by this tragical scene some pagods ran to the spot. They carried the princess to her couch and gave her every assistance. Imagination cannot paint the distress of Uglinette when she returned to her senses. How did she reproach herself for the affliction she had brought upon her husband. She loved him tenderly but she was horrified at his form and would have cheerfully given half the remainder of her days never to have seen him.

In the midst of her despair the fairy Magotine appeared. With a stroke of her wand she dissolved all the superb edifices, the charming gardens, the woods and meadows and fountains—all vanished into thin air. The wicked fairy gloated over the unfortunate queen and then said: "Well, madam, you are to set the whole world an example of patience which it will be difficult to imitate."

Uglinette waited in sorrow and terror while Magotine again waved her wand. There appeared a pair of iron shoes so small that Uglinette could not get half her foot into either of them, but notwithstanding that she was compelled to put them on. The poor queen could only weep and suffer.

"Here," said Magotine, "here is a spindle full of spider web. I expect you to spin it as fine as your hair and I give you but two hours to do it in."

"I have never spun, madam," said the queen, "but though what you desire appears to me to be impossible I will endeavor to obey you."

Magotine led her into the depths of a very dark grotto, the entrance to which she closed with a great stone. In trying to spin this filthy spider web Uglinette dropped her too heavy spindle a hundred times. She had the patience to pick it up again each time and to begin her work over again, but it was always in vain.

"Clearly do I see now," she said, "the extent of

my misery. I am consigned to the power of the implacable Magotine. Not satisfied with having deprived me of all my beauty she would find some pretext to kill me." She began to weep, recalling the happiness she enjoyed in the kingdom of Pagodia. Casting away her spindle she exclaimed: "Let Magotine come when she will! I cannot do impossibilities."

A voice answered her: "Ah, queen, your too imprudent curiosity has caused you these tears, but one cannot see those suffer whom we love. I have a friend whom I have not told you of before. She is called the fairy Protectrice. I trust she will be of great service to you." Immediately she heard three taps and without seeing anyone, she found her web spun and wound into a skein.

At the expiration of the two hours Magotine had the stone rolled from the mouth of the grotto and entered it. "Come, come," said the fairy, "let me see your work."

"Madam," said the queen, "it is quite true I did not know how to spin but I was obliged to learn."

When Magotine saw the extraordinary result she took the skein of spider web and said: "Truly, you are too skilful. It would be a great pity not to keep you employed. Here, queen, make me some nets with this thread strong enough to catch salmon in."

"Nay, for mercy's sake," replied the queen, "remember that it is barely strong enough to hold flies." In spite of her protests Magotine left the grotto and had the stone replaced, assuring her that if the nets were not finished in two hours she was a lost creature.

"Oh, fairy Protectrice!" exclaimed the queen. "If it be true that my sorrows can move your pity do not deny me your assistance." As she spoke the nets were made. Uglinette was extremely surprised and thanked the friendly fairy with all her heart. She reflected with delight that it was undoubtedly her husband who had secured for her such a friend.

"Alas, green dragon," she said, "you are very generous to continue to love me after the injuries I have done you." No reply was made for just then Magotine entered and was much astonished to find the nets so exceedingly well made.

"What!" she cried. "Will you have the audacity to maintain that you have woven these nets?"

"I have no friend in your court, madam," said the queen. "And even if I had, I am so carefully imprisoned that it would be difficult for anyone to speak to me without your permission."

"As you are so clever and skilful," said Magotine spitefully, "you will be of great use to me in my kingdom."

Magotine immediately ordered a ship and had the queen heavily chained down on its deck, fearing that in some fit of despair she might fling herself overboard. One night as the unhappy princess was deploring her sad fate, she saw by the light of the stars the green dragon quietly approaching the vessel over the waves.

"I am always afraid of alarming you," he said as he reached the ship, "and despite the reasons I have for not sparing you, you are infinitely dear to me."

"Can you pardon my imprudent curiosity?"

Uglinette asked him. "Is it really thou, love? Art thou again near? Dare I hope to have you again as my fond husband? Oh, how much I have suffered since I parted from thee!"

The green dragon was touched by her words and said: "When two who truly love have to part it brings much pain, even though we have a faint hope of meeting again." And he went on talking to her gently and lovingly.

Magotine was not one of those fairies who occasionally sleep. The desire to make mischief kept her continually awake. She did not fail to overhear the conversation between the dragon king and his wife, and she flew like a fury to interrupt it.

"Aha!" she cried. "You will talk, will you? I am delighted to hear you complain of your fate. Proserpine, who is my best friend, has begged me to send her a dragon. Green dragon, I command thee to go and finish thy penance in the shades and to give my compliments to the gentle Proserpine."

The unfortunate dragon king departed, uttering prolonged sighs and leaving the queen in the deepest affliction. She felt she had no longer anything to care for and in her despair exclaimed: "By what crime have we offended thee, Magotine? I was scarcely born when thy fiendish malediction robbed me of my beauty and rendered me ugly. Canst thou accuse me of any crime, when I had not at that time attained the use of reason? When I did not know myself? I am convinced that the unhappy king, whom thou hast just sent to the infernal regions, is as innocent as I was. But finish thy work and give me instant death. It is the only favor I ask of thee."

"Thou wouldst be too happy if I granted thy prayer," said Magotine. "Thou must first fetch me the four-leaf clovers that grow upon the Dragon's Hill, and draw for me the water of discretion from the bottomless spring."

As soon as the ship reached land, the cruel Magotine took a millstone and tied it around the queen's neck, ordering her to ascend with it to the summit of the Dragon's Mountain which soared high above the clouds. When there she was to gather enough four-leaf clovers to fill a basket, and then she was to descend into the depths of the valley and draw the water of discretion in a pitcher with a hole in the bottom of it and bring Magotine as much as would fill her large glass.

The queen said it was not in her power to obey her; that the millstone was more than ten times her own weight; and that she could not attempt anything so impossible.

"If thou dost not," said Magotine, "rest assured thy green dragon shall suffer for it."

This threat so frightened the queen that without thinking of the millstone she attempted to walk. But the effort would have been idle if the fairy Protectrice had not come to her assistance.

"Behold the just punishment of your fatal curiosity," said the fairy. "Blame no one but yourself for the state to which Magotine has reduced you."

So saying, the fairy Protectrice transported the poor queen to the top of the mountain and filled her basket for her with four-leaf clovers. The terrible monsters that guarded the spot tried to prevent her, but a tap of the fairy's wand rendered them as gentle as lambs.

The fairy Protectrice did not wait for the grateful queen to thank her but gave her a little car drawn by two white canaries, who spoke and whistled beautifully. She told Uglinette to descend the mountain and to fling her iron shoes at the two giants armed with clubs who guarded the fountain. They would thereupon fall senseless and she must then give her pitcher to the little canaries who would easily find means to fill it with the water of discretion. As soon as she was in possession of the water she should wash her face with it and she would become the most beautiful person in the world. She also advised Uglinette not to remain at the fountain nor to reascend the hill, but to stop in a very pleasant little grove she would find on her road. There she might remain for three years, as Magotine would only imagine that she was endeavoring to fill her pitcher with water, or that she had fallen a victim to some of the other perils of the journey.

The queen embraced the knees of the fairy Protectrice and thanked her a hundred times for the special favors she had conferred on her. "But," added the queen, "neither the success I may achieve, nor the beauty which you promise me can give me the least pleasure until my green dragon is released from his penance."

"That will not be," said the fairy, "until you have passed three years in the mountain grove and have returned to Magotine with the four-leaf clovers and the water in the leaky pitcher."

The queen promised the fairy Protectrice that

she would carefully follow her directions. "But, madam," she added, "shall I be three years without hearing tidings of my green dragon?"

"You deserve never to hear of him again as long as you live," said the fairy. "Can anything be more shocking than to have caused him to recommence his penance?"

The queen made no reply; the tears that flowed down her cheeks and her silence sufficiently proved the pain she suffered. She got into her little car and the canaries did their duty. They conducted her to the bottom of the valley where the giants guarded the fountain of discretion. She quickly took off her iron shoes and threw them at their heads. The moment the shoes touched them they fell lifeless as colossal statues to the ground. The canaries took the leaky pitcher and mended it with such skill that there was no appearance of its having ever been broken. They filled it with the water of discretion and brought it back to the queen. The name given to the water made her anxious to drink some of it.

"It will make me more prudent and discreet than I have been," she reflected. "Alas, if I had possessed those qualities I should still be in the kingdom of Pagodia." After she had drunk a long draught of the water she washed her face with some of it and became so beautiful that she seemed more a goddess than a mortal.

The fairy Protectrice immediately appeared and said to her: "You have just done that which has pleased me exceedingly. You knew that this water could embellish your mind as well as your person. I wished to see to which of the two you would give the preference and it has been to your mind. I praise you for it and this act will shorten the term of your punishment."

"Diminish none of my sufferings," replied the queen. "I deserve them all. But comfort green dragon who deserves none of his."

"I will do all in my power," said the fairy, embracing her. "But since you are now so beautiful I desire you will drop the name Uglinette, which no longer suits you. You must be called Queen Discrète."

So saying the fairy vanished, leaving the queen a pair of pretty little shoes, so beautifully embroidered that they delighted her heart.

When she re-entered the car with her pitcher full of water, the canaries flew with her straight to the grove of the mountain. There never was a more agreeable spot. The myrtle and orange trees interlaced their branches to form long covered walks and bowers into which the sun could not penetrate. A thousand rills from gently flowing fountains shed a refreshing coolness through this beautiful abode. But what was most curious all the animals in it spoke and gave the warmest welcome in the world to the little canaries.

"We thought you had deserted us," they said.

"The term of our penance is not yet completed," replied the canaries, "but here is a queen whom the fairy Protectrice has ordered us to bring to you. Take all the pains you can to amuse her."

She was immediately surrounded by all sorts of animals who paid her their best compliments. "You shall be our queen," they said to her. "You shall find no attention or respect wanting on our parts."

"Where am I?" the queen exclaimed. "By what supernatural power are you enabled to speak to me?"

One of the little canary birds who had remained beside her whispered in her ear: "You must know, madam, that several fairies being on their travels were distressed to see persons fall into bad habits. They at first imagined it would be sufficient to advise them to correct themselves, but their warnings were in vain and becoming at length quite vexed with them they imposed penances upon them. Some who talked too much they changed into parrots, magpies and hens. Those who ridiculed their friends, into monkeys. Greedy persons into pigs, and hot-headed people into lions. In short, the number of persons they made to do penance was so great that this grove is full of them, and you will therefore find in it folk of all qualities and dispositions."

This information interested Queen Discrète, and several of the birds and animals offered to relate the reasons for their penances whenever she pleased. She thanked them very politely but as she felt more inclined to muse than to talk, she sought a secluded spot where she could remain alone. As soon as she had chosen one a little palace arose on it and the most sumptuous banquet in the world was served up to her. It consisted only of fruits but they were of the rarest description. They were brought to her by birds and during her stay in the grove she wanted for nothing.

There were entertainments occasionally which pleased her more from their singularity than anything else. Lions were seen to dance with lambs. Bears whispered tender things to doves, and butterflies fluttered around the heads of panthers. In short, there was no classification of species for it was not that one was a tiger and another a sheep, but simply that they were persons whom the fairies had chosen to punish for their faults.

They all loved Queen Discrète to adoration. Everyone made her his umpire in any difference. Her power was absolute in this little republic and if she had not continually reproached herself as the cause of the green dragon's misfortunes, she might have borne her own with some degree of patience. But when she thought of the state to which he was reduced, she could not forgive herself for her inprudent curiosity.

The time at last arrived for her to leave the grove and the faithful little canaries conducted her out of the happy spot. She left secretly in the night-time to avoid the leave takings and lamentations which would have cost her some tears, for she was affected by the friendship and respect which all these enchanted animals had testified for her.

She forgot neither the pitcher full of the water of discretion, nor the basket of four-leaf clovers, nor the iron shoes. At the moment when Magotine believed her to be dead, she presented herself suddenly before her, the millstone round her neck, the iron shos on her feet, and the pitcher in her hand. The fairy uttered a loud cry at the sight of her, and then inquired whence she came.

"Madam," said the queen, "I have passed three

years drawing water in the broken pitcher, at the end of which time I found the way to make it hold water."

Magotine laughed loudly at this, thinking of the fatigue the poor queen must have undergone. But looking at her more attentively she exclaimed: "What's this I see! Uglinette has become quite lovely! How came you by this beauty?"

The queen informed her that she had washed herself with the water of discretion and that this miracle had been the result. At these words Magotine dashed the pitcher to the ground. "Oh, thou power that defiest me!" she exclaimed. "I will be revenged. Get your iron shoes ready," she said to the queen. "You must go for me to the infernal regions and demand of Proserpine the essence of long life. I am always afraid of falling sick and perhaps dying. When I have this antidote I shall have no more fear. Take care that you do not uncork the bottle nor taste the liquid she gives you or you will diminish my portion."

The poor queen had never been so astonished as she was by this order. "Which is the way to the infernal regions?" she asked. "Can those who go to them return? Alas, Madam, will you never weary of persecuting me?"

She began to weep and Magotine, exulting at the sight of her tears, laughed loudly and exclaimed: "Go, go! Do not delay a moment your departure on a voyage from which I shall reap so much gratification." She filled for her a wallet with old nuts and stale rye bread and with this the poor queen started out, determined to dash her brains out against the first rock she came to and thus end her sorrows.

She walked for some time, turning now one way and then another, thinking it was a great hardship to be sent thus to the infernal regions. When she was tired she lay down at the foot of a tree and began to think of the poor dragon king, forgetting all about her own journey. Suddenly she beheld the fairy Protectrice who said to her: "Know you not, beautiful queen, that to release your husband from the shades in which the commands of the Magotine detain him, it is necessary you should seek the home of Proserpine?"

"I would go much farther if it were possible, madam," she replied, "but I do not know the way by which I can descend into that dark abode."

"Here is a green branch," said the fairy. "Strike the earth with it and repeat these lines distinctly." The queen embraced the knees of her generous friend and then said after her:

> Love, listen to my prayer!
> Come, save me from despair.
> Calm the pangs that tear my heart
> And lead me to those realms apart
> Where Proserpine resides.

She had scarcely finished when a beautiful young child appeared in the midst of a blue and gold cloud, a crown of flowers encircling his brow. He flew down at her feet and the queen knew by his bow and arrows that it was Love. He spoke to her gently, and promised her everything would be all right.

The queen was dazzled at the splendor that surrounded Love and thrilled with delight at his promises. She exclaimed: "I'll follow thee without fear, O Cupid! I'll go with thee to the realms of woe where my love is."

Love struck the earth three times with his bow, singing as he did so:

Earth, my voice obey!
The power of Cupid own!
Open for Love the way
To Proserpine's home.

The earth obeyed and there appeared a dark passage in which the queen needed a guide as shining as the God of Love. She dreaded meeting her husband under the form of a dragon, but Love had foreseen this and had already ordered that the green dragon should become what he was previous to his penance.

Powerful as Magotine was what could she do against Love? The first sight that met the queen's eyes was her husband, now a handsome young prince. She had not seen him thus nor had he beheld her in her beauty, but Love made each of them know who the other was. The queen said to him tenderly: "I have come to share thy prison and penance. Even this dark realm hath no terrors for me if we are united here."

The king, transported by the sight of his beautiful wife, said everything that could prove his ardor and delight. But Love, who is not fond of losing time, urged them to approach Proserpine. The queen gave her Magotine's compliments and requested she would intrust her with the essence of long life. It was the watchword between these two people and Proserpine immediately gave the queen a phial very badly corked, in order to induce her to open it.

Love, who is ever watchful, warned the queen against a curiosity which would again be fatal to her, and quickly leaving the gloomy halls of Proserpine the king and queen returned to the light of day. Love did not abandon them but led them back to Magotine. In order that she might not see him, he hid himself in their hearts, but his presence nevertheless inspired the fairy with such humane sentiments that although she knew not the reason, she received the king and queen very graciously.

With a supernatural effort of generosity she restored to them the kingdom of Pagodia. They returned to it immediately and passed the rest of their days there in as much happiness as they had previously endured afflictions and trials.

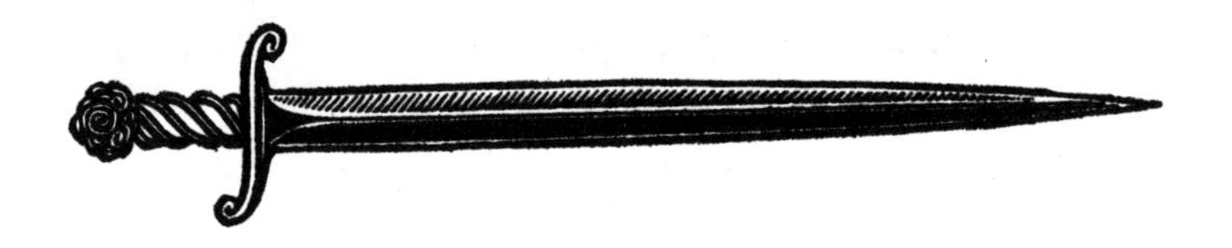

The Dragon-Princess

CHINESE

IN the Sea of Dungting there is a hill, and in that hill there is a hole, and this hole is so deep that it has no bottom.

Once a fisherman who was passing there, slipped and fell into the hole. He came to a country full of winding ways which led over hill and dale for several miles. Finally he reached a dragon-castle lying in a great plain around which grew a green slime which reached to his knees. He went up to the gate of the castle which was guarded by a dragon who spouted water which dispersed in a fine mist. Within the gate lay a small hornless dragon who raised his head, showed his claws, and would not let him in.

The fisherman spent several days in the cave, satisfying his hunger with the green slime, which he found edible and which tasted like rice-mush. At last he found a way out again and went home. He told the district mandarin what had happened to him, and the latter reported the matter to the emperor. The emperor sent for a wise man and questioned him concerning it.

The wise man said: "There are four paths in this cave. One path leads to the south-west shore of the Sea of Dungting; the second path leads to a valley in the land of the four rivers; the third path ends in a cave on the mountain of Lo-Fu; and the fourth in an island of the Eastern Sea. In this cave dwells the seventh daughter of the Dragon-King of the Eastern Sea, who guards his pearls and his treasure. It happened once in the ancient days, that a fisherboy dived into the water and brought up a pearl from beneath the chin of a black dragon. The dragon was asleep, which was the reason the fisherboy brought the pearl to the surface without being harmed. The treasure which the daughter of the Dragon-King has in charge is made up of thousands and millions of such jewels. Several thousands of small dragons watch over them in her service, but these dragons dislike wax. They are fond of beautiful jade-stones, and of kung-tsing, the hollowgreen wood, and like to eat swallows. If one were to send a messenger with a letter, it would be possible to obtain precious pearls."

The emperor was greatly pleased, and announced a large reward for the man who was competent to go to the dragon-castle as his messenger.

The first man to come forward was named So Pi-Lo. But the wise man said: "A great-great-great-great-grandfather of yours once slew more than a hundred of the dragons of the Eastern Sea, and was finally himself slain by the dragons. The dragons are the enemies of your family and you cannot go."

Then came a man from Canton, Lo-Dsi-Tschun, with his two brothers, who said that his ancestors had been related to the Dragon-King. Hence they were well liked by the dragons and well known to them. They begged to be entrusted with the message.

The wise man asked: "And have you will in your possession the stone which compels the dragons to do your will?"

"Yes," said they, "we have brought it along with us."

The wise man had them show him the stone; then he spoke: "This stone is only obeyed by the dragons who make clouds and send down the rain. It will not do for the dragons who guard the pearls of the sea-king." Then he questioned them further: "Have you the dragon-brain vapor?"

When they admitted that they had not, the wise man said: "How then will you compel the dragons to yield their treasure?"

And the emperor said: "What shall we do?"

The wise man replied: "On the Western Ocean sail foreign merchants who deal in dragon-brain vapor. Some one must go to them and seek it from them. I also know a holy man who is an adept in the art of taming dragons, and who has prepared ten pounds of the dragon-stone. Some one should be sent for that as well."

The emperor sent out his messengers. They met

one of the holy man's disciples and obtained two fragments of dragon-stone from him.

Said the wise man: "This is what we want!"

Several more months went by, and at last a pill of dragon-brain vapor had also been secured. The emperor felt much pleased and had his jewelers carve two little boxes of the finest jade. These were polished with the ashes of the Wutung-tree. And he had an essence prepared of the very best hollowgreen wood, pasted with sea-fish lime, and hardened in the fire. Of this two vases were made. Then the bodies and the clothing of the messengers were rubbed with tree-wax, and they were given five hundred roasted swallows to take along with them.

They went into the cave. When they reached the dragon-castle, the little dragon who guarded the gate smelled the tree-wax, so he crouched down and did them no harm. They gave him a hundred roasted swallows as a bribe to announce them to the daughter of the Dragon-King. They were admitted to her presence and offered her the jade caskets, the vases and the four hundred roasted swallows as gifts. The dragon's daughter received them graciously, and they unfolded the emperor's letter.

In the castle there was a dragon who was over a thousand years old. He could turn himself into a human being, and could interpret the language of human beings. Through him the dragon's daughter learned that the emperor was sending her the gifts, and she returned them with a gift of three great pearls, seven smaller pearls and a whole bushel of ordinary pearls. The messengers took leave, rode off with their pearls on a dragon's back, and in a moment they had reached the banks of the Yangtze-kiang. They made their way to Nanking, the imperial capital, and there handed over their treasure of gems.

The emperor was much pleased and showed them to the wise man. He said: "Of the three great pearls one is a divine wishing-pearl of the third class, and two are black dragon-pearls of medium quality. Of the seven smaller pearls two are serpent-pearls, and five are mussel-pearls. The remaining pearls are in part sea-crane pearls, in part snail and oyster-pearls. They do not approach the great pearls in value, and yet few will be found to equal them on earth."

The emperor also showed them to all his servants. They, however, thought the wise man's words all talk, and did not believe what he said.

Then the wise man said: "The radiance of wishing-pearls of the first class is visible for forty miles, that of the second class for twenty miles, that of the third class for ten miles. As far as their radiance carries, neither wind nor rain, thunder nor lightning, water, fire nor weapons may reach. The pearls of the black dragon are nine-colored and glow by night. Within the circle of their light the poison of serpents and worms is powerless. The serpent-pearls are seven-colored, the mussel-pearls are five-colored. Both shine by night. Those most free from spots are the best. They grow within the mussel, and increase and decrease in size as the moon waxes and wanes."

Some one asked how the serpent- and sea-crane pearls could be told apart, and the wise man answered: "The animals themselves recognize them."

Then the emperor selected a serpent-pearl and a sea-crane pearl, put them together with a whole bushel of ordinary pearls, and poured the lot out in the courtyard. Then a large yellow serpent and a black crane were fetched and placed among the pearls. At once the crane took up a sea-crane pearl in his bill and began to dance and sing and flutter around. But the serpent snatched at the serpent-pearl, and wound himself about it in many coils. And when the people saw this they acknowledged the truth of the wise man's words. As regards the radiance of the larger and smaller pearls it turned out, too, just as the wise man had said.

In the dragon-castle the messengers had enjoyed dainty fare, which tasted like flowers, herbs, ointment and sugar. They had brought a remnant of it with them to the capital; yet exposed to the air it had become as hard as stone. The emperor commanded that these fragments be preserved in the treasury. Then he bestowed high rank and titles on the three brothers, and made each one of them a present of a thousand rolls of fine silk stuff. He also learned why it was that the fisherman, when he chanced upon the cave, had not been destroyed by the dragons. It turned out that the fisherman's clothes had been soaked in oil and tree-wax, and the dragons had dreaded the odor, so they let him pass unharmed.

The Dragon of the North

ANDREW LANG

VERY long ago, as old people have told me, there lived a terrible monster who came out of the North and laid waste whole tracts of country, devouring both men and beasts; and this monster was so destructive that it was feared that unless help came no living creature would be left on the face of the earth. It had a body like an ox and legs like a frog, two short fore legs and two long ones behind, and besides that it had a tail like a serpent ten fathoms in length. When it moved it jumped like a frog, and with every spring it covered half a mile of ground. Fortunately its habit was to remain for several years in the same place, and not to move on till the whole neighborhood was eaten up. Nothing could hurt it, because its whole body was covered with scales which were harder than stone or metal; its two great eyes shone by night and even by day, like the brightest lamps, and any one who had the ill-luck to look into those eyes became as it were bewitched and was obliged to rush of his own accord into the monster's jaws. In this way the dragon was able to feed upon both men and beasts without the least trouble to itself, as it needed not to move from the spot where it was lying.

All the neighboring kings had offered rich rewards to any one who should be able to destroy the monster, either by force or enchantment, and many had tried their luck, but all had miserably failed. Once a great forest was burned down, but the fire did not do the monster the least harm. However, there was a tradition among the wise men of the country that the dragon might be overcome by one who possessed King Solomon's signet ring, upon which a secret writing was engraved. This inscription would enable any one who was wise enough to interpret it to find out how the dragon could be destroyed. Only no one knew where the ring was hidden, nor was there any sorcerer or learned man to be found who would be able to explain the inscription.

At last a young man, with a good heart and plenty of courage, set out to search for the ring. He took his way toward the sun-rising, because he knew that all the wisdom of old times comes from the East. After some years he met with a famous Eastern magician and asked for his advice in the matter. The magician answered:

"Mortal men have but little wisdom and can give you no help, but the birds of the air would be better guides to you if you could learn their language.

I can help you to understand it if you will stay with me a few days."

The youth thankfully accepted the magician's offer and said: "I cannot now offer you any reward for your kindness, but should my undertaking succeed your trouble shall be richly repaid."

Then the magician brewed a powerful potion out of nine sorts of herbs which he had gathered himself all alone by moonlight, and he gave the youth nine spoonfuls of it daily for three days, which made him able to understand the language of birds.

At parting the magician said to him: "If you ever find Solomon's ring and get possession of it, then come back to me, that I may explain the inscription on the ring to you, for there is no one else in the world who can do this."

From that time the youth never felt lonely as he walked along; he always had company, because he understood the language of birds; and in this way he learned many things which mere human knowledge could never have taught him. But time went on and he heard nothing about the ring. It happened one evening, when he was hot and tired with walking and had sat down under a tree in a forest to eat his supper, that he saw two gayly plumaged birds that were strange to him sitting at the top of the tree talking to one another about him. The first bird said:

"I know that wandering fool under the tree there, who has come so far without finding what he seeks. He is trying to find King Solomon's lost ring."

The old bird answered: "He will have to seek help from the witch maiden, who will doubtless be able to put him on the right track. If she has not got the ring herself she knows well enough who has it."

"But where is he to find the witch maiden?" said the first bird. "She has no settled dwelling, but is here to-day and gone to-morrow. He might as well try to catch the wind."

The other replied: "I do not know, certainly, where she is at present, but in three nights from now she will come to the spring to wash her face, as she does every month when the moon is full, in order that she may never grow old or wrinkled, but may always keep the bloom of youth."

"Well," said the first bird, "the spring is not far from here. Shall we go and see how it is she does it?"

"Willingly, if you like," said the other.

The youth immediately resolved to follow the birds to the spring, only two things made him uneasy: first, lest he might be asleep when the birds went, and, secondly, lest he might lose sight of them, since he had not wings to carry him along so swiftly. He was too tired to keep awake all night, yet his anxiety prevented him from sleeping soundly, and when with the earliest dawn he looked up to the tree-top, he was glad to see his feathered companions still asleep with their heads under their wings. He ate his breakfast and waited until the birds should start, but they did not leave the place all day. They hopped about from one tree to another looking for food all day long until the evening, when they went back to their old perch to sleep.

The next day the same thing happened, but on the third morning one bird said to the other: "To-day we must go to the spring to see the witch maiden wash her face." They remained on the tree till noon; then they flew away and went toward the South. The young man's heart beat with anxiety lest he should lose sight of his guides, but he managed to keep the birds in view until they again perched upon a tree.

The young man ran after them until he was quite exhausted and out of breath, and after three short rests the birds at length reached a small open space in the forest, on the edge of which they placed themselves on the top of a high tree. When the youth had overtaken them he saw that there was a clear spring in the middle of the space. He sat down at the foot of the tree upon which the birds were perched and listened attentively to what they were saying to each other.

"The sun is not down yet," said the first bird. "We must wait yet awhile till the moon rises and the maiden comes to the spring. Do you think she will see that young man sitting under the tree?"

"Nothing is likely to escape her eyes, certainly not a young man," said the other bird. "Will the youth have the sense not to let himself be caught in her toils?"

"We will wait," said the first bird, "and see how they get on together."

The evening light had quite faded and the full moon was already shining down upon the forest when the young man heard a slight rustling sound. After a few moments there came out of the forest a maiden, gliding over the grass so lightly that her feet seemed scarcely to touch the ground, and stood beside the spring. The youth could not turn away his eyes from the maiden, for he had never in his life seen a woman so beautiful. Without seeming to notice anything, she went to the spring, looked up to the full moon, then knelt down and bathed her face nine times, then looked up to the moon again and walked nine times round the well, and as she walked she sang this song:

Full-faced moon with light unshaded,
Let my beauty ne'er be faded.
Never let my cheek grow pale!
While the moon is waning nightly,
May the maiden bloom more brightly,
May her freshness never fail!

Then she dried her face with her long hair and was about to go away, when her eye suddenly fell upon the spot where the young man was sitting, and she turned toward the tree. The youth rose and stood waiting. Then the maiden said:

"You ought to have a heavy punishment because you have presumed to watch my secret doings in the moonlight. But I will forgive you this time, because you are a stranger and knew no better. But you must tell me truly who you are and how you came to this place, where no mortal has ever set foot before."

The youth answered humbly: "Forgive me, beautiful maiden, if I have unintentionally offended you. I chanced to come here after long wandering, and found a good place to sleep under this tree. At your coming I did not know what to do, but stayed where I was, because I thought my silent watching could not offend you."

The maiden answered kindly: "Come and spend

this night with us. You will sleep better on a pillow than on damp moss."

The youth hesitated for a little, but presently he heard the birds saying from the top of the tree: "Go where she calls you, but take care to give no blood, or you will sell your soul." So the youth went with her, and soon they reached a beautiful garden, where stood a splendid house, which glittered in the moonlight as if it was all built out of gold and silver. When the youth entered he found many splendid chambers, each one finer than the last. Hundreds of tapers burned upon golden candlesticks and shed a light like the brightest day.

At length they reached a chamber where a table was spread with the most costly dishes. At the table were placed two chairs, one of silver, the other of gold. The maiden seated herself upon the golden chair and offered the silver one to her companion. They were served by maidens dressed in white, whose feet made no sound as they moved about, and not a word was spoken during the meal. Afterward the youth and the witch maiden conversed pleasantly together until a woman, dressed in red, came in to remind them that it was bedtime. The youth was now shown into another room containing a silken bed with down cushions, where he slept delightfully, yet he seemed to hear a voice near his bed which repeated to him: "Remember to give no blood!"

The next morning the maiden asked him whether he would not like to stay with her always in this beautiful place, and as he did not answer immediately she continued: "You see how I always remain young and beautiful, and I am under no one's orders, but can do just what I like, so that I have never thought of marrying before. But from the moment I saw you I took a fancy to you, so if you agree we might be married and might live together like princes, because I have great riches."

The youth could not but be tempted with the beautiful maiden's offer, but he remembered how the birds had called her the witch, and their warning always sounded in his ears. Therefore he answered cautiously: "Do not be angry, dear maiden, if I do not decide immediately on this important matter. Give me a few days to consider before we come to an understanding."

"Why not?" answered the maiden. "Take some weeks to consider if you like, and take counsel with your own heart." And to make the time pass pleasantly, she took the youth over every part of her beautiful dwelling and showed him all her splendid treasures. But these treasures were all produced by enchantment, for the maiden could make anything she wished appear by the help of King Solomon's signet ring; only none of these things remained fixed; they passed away like the wind without leaving a trace behind. But the youth did not know this; he thought they were all real.

One day the maiden took him into a secret chamber, where a little gold box was standing on a silver table. Pointing to the box she said: "Here is my greatest treasure, whose like is not to be found in the whole world. It is a precious gold ring. When you marry me I will give you this ring as a marriage gift, and it will make you the happiest of mortal men. But in order that our love may last forever, you must give me for the ring three drops of blood from the little finger of your left hand."

When the youth heard these words a cold shudder ran over him, for he remembered that his soul was at stake. He was cunning enough, however, to conceal his feelings and to make no direct answer, but he only asked the maiden, as if carelessly, what was remarkable about the ring.

She answered: "No mortal is able entirely to understand the power of this ring, because no one thoroughly understands the secret signs engraved upon it. But even with my half-knowledge I can work great wonders. If I put the ring upon the little finger of my left hand, then I can fly like a bird through the air wherever I wish to go. If I put it on the third finger of my left hand I am invisible, and I can see everything that passes around me, though no one can see me. If I put the ring upon the middle finger of my left hand, then neither fire nor water nor any sharp weapon can hurt me. If I put it on the forefinger of my left hand, then I can with its help produce whatever I wish. I can in a single moment build houses or anything I desire. Finally, as long as I wear the ring on the thumb of my left hand, that hand is so strong that it can break down rocks and walls. Besides these, the ring has other secret signs which, as I said, no one can understand. No doubt it contains secrets of great importance. The ring formerly belonged to King Solomon, the wisest of kings, during whose reign the wisest men lived. But it is not known whether this ring was ever made by mortal hands: it is supposed that an angel gave it to the wise king."

When the youth heard all this he determined to try and get possession of the ring, though he did not quite believe in all its wonderful gifts. He wished the maiden would let him have it in his hand, but he did not quite like to ask her to do so, and after awhile she put it back into the box. A few days after they were again speaking of the magic ring, and the youth said: "I do not think it possible that the ring can have all the power you say it has."

Then the maiden opened the box and took the ring out, and it glittered as she held it like the clearest sunbeam. She put it on the middle finger of her left hand, and told the youth to take a knife and try as hard as he could to cut her with it, for he would not be able to hurt her. He was unwilling at first, but the maiden insisted. Then he tried, at first only in play, and then seriously, to strike her with the knife, but an invisible wall of iron seemed to be between them, and the maiden stood before him laughing and unhurt. Then she put the ring on her third finger and in an instant she had vanished from his eyes. Presently she was beside him again laughing and holding the ring between her fingers.

"Do let me try," said the youth, "whether I can do these wonderful things."

The maiden, suspecting no treachery, gave him the magic ring.

The youth pretended to have forgotten what to do, and asked what finger he must put the ring on so that no sharp weapon could hurt him.

"Oh, the middle finger of your left hand," the maiden answered, laughing.

She took the knife and tried to strike the youth,

and he even tried to cut himself with it, but found it impossible. Then he asked the maiden to show him how to split stones and rocks with the help of the ring. So she led him into a courtyard where stood a great boulder. "Now," she said, "put the ring upon the thumb of your left hand, and you will see how strong that hand has become." The youth did so, and found to his astonishment that with a single blow of his fist the stone flew into a thousand pieces. Then the youth bethought him that he who does not use his luck when he has it is a fool, and that this was a chance which once lost might never return. So while they stood laughing at the shattered stone he placed the ring, as if in play, upon the third finger of his left hand.

"Now," said the maiden, "you are invisible to me until you take the ring off again."

But the youth had no mind to do that. On the contrary, he went further off, then put the ring on the little finger of his left hand, and soared into the air like a bird.

When the maiden saw him flying away she thought at first that he was still in play and cried: "Come back, friend, for now you see I have told you the truth." But the young man never came back.

Then the maiden saw she was deceived, and bitterly repented that she had ever trusted him with the ring.

The young man never halted in his flight until he reached the dwelling of the wise magician who had taught him the speech of birds. The magician was delighted to find that his search had been successful, and at once set to work to interpret the secret signs engraved upon the ring, but it took him seven weeks to make them out clearly. Then he gave the youth the following instructions how to overcome the dragon of the North:

"You must have an iron horse cast, which must have little wheels under each foot. You must also be armed with a spear two fathoms long, which you will be able to wield by means of the magic ring upon your left thumb. The spear must be as thick in the middle as a large tree, and both its ends must be sharp. In the middle of the spear you must have two strong chains ten fathoms in length. As soon as the dragon has made himself fast to the spear, which you must thrust through his jaws, you must spring quickly from the iron horse and fasten the ends of the chains firmly to the ground with iron stakes, so that he cannot get away from them. After two or three days the monster's strength will be so far exhausted that you will be able to come near him. Then you can put Solomon's ring upon your left thumb and give him the finishing strike, but keep the ring on your third finger until you have come close to him, so that the monster cannot see you, else he might strike you dead with his long tail. But when all is done, take care you do not lose the ring and that no one takes it from you by cunning."

The young man thanked the magician for his directions, and promised, should they succeed, to reward him. But the magician answered: "I have profited so much by the wisdom the ring has taught me that I desire no other reward." Then they parted, and the youth quickly flew home through the air. After remaining in his own home for some weeks he heard people say that the terrible dragon of the North was not far off and might shortly be expected in the country. The king announced publicly that he would give his daughter in marriage, as well as a large part of his kingdom, to whosoever should free the country from the monster.

The youth then went to the king and told him that he had good hopes of subduing the dragon if the king would grant him all he desired for that purpose. The king willingly agreed, and the iron horse, the great spear, and the chains were all prepared as the youth requested. When all was ready, it was found that the iron horse was so heavy that a hundred men could not move it from the spot, so the youth found there was nothing for it but to move it with his own strength by means of the magic ring. The dragon was now so near that in a couple of springs he would be over the frontier. The youth now began to consider how he should act, for if he had to push the iron horse from behind he could not ride upon it as the sorcerer had said he must. But a raven unexpectedly gave him this advice: "Ride upon the horse and push the spear against the ground, as if you were pushing off a boat from the land."

The youth did so, and found that in this way he could easily move forward. The dragon had his monstrous jaws wide open, all ready for his expected prey. A few paces nearer, and man and horse would have been swallowed up by them! The youth trembled with horror and his blood ran cold, yet he did not lose his courage; but holding the iron spear upright in his hand, he brought it down with all his might right through the monster's lower jaw. Then quick as lightning he sprang from his horse before the dragon had time to shut his mouth. A fearful clap of thunder, which could be heard for miles around, now warned him that the dragon's jaws had closed upon the spear.

When the youth turned round he saw the point of the spear sticking up high above the dragon's upper jaw and knew that the other end must be fastened firmly to the ground; but the dragon had got his teeth fixed in the iron horse, which was now useless. The youth now hastened to fasten down the chains to the ground by means of the enormous iron pegs which he had provided. The death struggle of the monster lasted three days and three nights; in his writhing he beat his tail so violently against the ground that at ten miles' distance the earth trembled as if with an earthquake. When he at length lost power to move his tail, the youth with the help of the ring took up a stone which twenty ordinary men could not have moved, and beat the dragon so hard about the head with it that very soon the monster lay lifeless before him.

You can fancy how great was the rejoicing when the news was spread abroad that the terrible monster was dead. His conqueror was received into the city with as much pomp as if he had been the mightiest of kings. The old king did not need to urge his daughter to marry the slayer of the dragon; he found her already willing to bestow her hand upon this hero, who had done all alone what whole armies had tried in vain to do.

In a few days a magnificent wedding was celebrated at which the rejoicing lasted four whole weeks, for all the neighboring kinds had met together to thank the man who had freed the world from their common enemy. But everyone forgot amid the general joy that they ought to have buried the dragon's monstrous body, for it began now to have such a bad smell that no one could live in the neighborhood, and before long the whole air was poisoned and pestilence broke out which destroyed many hundreds of people. In this distress, the king's son-in-law resolved to seek help once more from the Eastern magician, to whom he at once traveled through the air like a bird by the help of the ring.

But there is a proverb which says that ill-gotten gains never prosper, and the prince found that the stolen ring brought him ill-luck after all. The witch maiden had never rested night or day until she had found out where the ring was. As soon as she had discovered by means of magical arts that the prince in the form of a bird was on his way to the Eastern magician, she changed herself into an eagle and watched in the air until the bird she was waiting for came in sight, for, she knew him at once by the ring which was hung round his neck by a ribbon. Then the eagle pounced upon the bird, and the moment she seized him in her talons she tore the ring from his neck before the man in bird's shape had time to prevent her. Then the eagle flew down to the earth with her prey, and the two stood face to face once more in human form.

"Now, villain, you are in my power!" cried the witch maiden. "I favored you with my love, and you repaid me with treachery and theft. You stole my most precious jewel from me, and do you expect to live happily as the king's son-in-law? Now the tables are turned; you are in my power, and I will be revenged on you for your crimes."

"Forgive me! forgive me!" cried the prince. "I know too well how deeply I have wronged you, and most heartily do I repent it."

The maiden answered: "Your prayers and your repentance come too late, and if I were to spare you everyone would think me a fool. You have doubly wronged me; first you scorned my love and then you stole my ring, and you must bear the punishment."

With these words she put the ring upon her left thumb, lifted the young man with one hand, and walked away with him under her arm. This time she did not take him to a splendid palace, but to a deep cave in a rock, where there were chains hanging from the wall. The maiden now chained the young man's hands and feet so that he could not escape; then she said in an angry voice: "Here you shall remain chained up until you die. I will bring you every day enough food to prevent you dying of hunger, but you need never hope for freedom any more." With these words she left him.

The old king and his daughter waited anxiously for many weeks for the prince's return, but no news of him arrived. The king's daughter often dreamed that her husband was going through some great suffering. She therefore begged her father to summon all the enchanters and magicians, that they might try to find out where the prince was and how he could be set free. But the magicians, with all their arts, could find out nothing, except that he was still living and undergoing great suffering, but none could tell where he was to be found. At last a celebrated magician from Finland was brought before the king, who had found out that the king's son-in-law was imprisoned in the East, not by men, but by some more powerful being. The king now sent messengers to the East to look for his son-in-law, and they by good luck met with the old magician who had interpreted the signs on King Solomon's ring, and thus was possessed of more wisdom than any one else in the world. The magician soon found out what he wished to know, and pointed out the place where the prince was imprisoned, but said: "He is kept there by enchantment and cannot be set free without my help. I will therefore go with you myself."

So they all set out, guided by birds, and after some days came to the cave where the unfortunate prince had been chained up for nearly seven years. He recognized the magician immediately, but the old man did not know him, he had grown so thin. However, he undid the chains by the help of magic and took care of the prince until he recovered and became strong enough to travel. When he reached home he found that the old king had died that morning, so that he was now raised to the throne. And now after his long suffering came prosperity, which lasted to the end of his life; but he never got back the magic ring, nor has it ever again been seen by mortal eyes.

Ragnar Shaggy-breeches

PHILIP SCHUYLER ALLEN

ENDLONG down the great hall at Hledra fires were kindled. It was evening, and sounds of merriment filled the palace. Ragnar the King sat enthroned under a golden canopy, while his warriors feasted in groups near the blazing logs. Maidens waited upon the men and filled their drinking horns with sparkling wine. Then a hush fell upon the assembly as the King's scald, or bard, arose and took his place before the King.

The scald sang of the warlike deeds of Ragnar, the boy king, famous in Denmark. How he had led the Danes in many a battle on foreign shores and always gained the day. Once had the Danes set forth in ships along the sea, where the wind raised mighty billows and drove them at last against the coast of Norway. In Norway, sang the scald, had the mighty

Ragnar fought against an army single-handed, and by his valor saved a warrior queen.

When the old man's song was done, his hearers were silent, remembering the battles they had seen. Then it was that a certain man entered the hall, unknown of aspect to the warriors there. To them he said he was a merchant from the East. A great pack he had, filled with wares from strange lands, and he asked permission to show these before the King.

Then the man showed the King a magic mirror, and, looking into the glass, Ragnar beheld an exceeding fair woman, like a burning flame to look upon, and he yearned above all things for her.

"The chieftain who possesses such a treasure," said the King, "must be the happiest man in all the North."

"Truly, O King," replied the stranger, "thou sayest well. The maiden in the mirror is a king's daughter. Herrod, of East Gothland, is her father. No woman fairer than she is may be found in all the world. So wise is she that her father seeks her counsel when setting out to war; and no man yet has conquered him in battle. But now she and her father are in great distress."

Then Ragnar asked the man how that might be, and the merchant told this tale:

Two warriors, returning to East Gothland rich in plunder, had made a present to the king's daughter of a griffin's egg, which they had won in war. At King Herrod's command the egg was hatched by a swan and out of it a winged serpent came. The Princess put the little creature in a golden cage and fed it with her own hands. But so quickly it grew that soon the monster was too large for the cage, and even for the room, and now it surrounded the whole house in which the Princess lived. The monster guarded her with a jealous eye, nor would he allow her to leave the house. No one dared touch him, for his eyes were like unto flaming fire, his breath was deadly poison, and with his tail he could break the strongest oak tree as easily as if it were a reed. To rid the land of this curse Herrod had promised the hand of his daughter to the warrior who should succeed in slaying the evil monster.

Such was the stranger's tale. And having finished, the unknown man departed from the hall, and none knew who he was or whither he went.

No sooner had Ragnar heard the tale to its end than he determined to slay the dragon himself. He ordered a garment of thick wool and oxhide, and this he dipped in tar; for well he knew that through such a garment neither poison nor venom could penetrate.

Then the King bade his men make ready the ships for the journey to East Gothland. At dawn they set sail and had wind at will. And Ragnar himself steered the greatest of the dragon-keels. Richly wrought were their sails and glorious to look upon. But when a few days were past, there arose a great storm on the sea, and the waves were dark to behold. Now there fell on the Danes so fierce a storm and so huge a sea, that the beat of the waves against the prows sounded like high hills clashing together. But Ragnar bade his men fear naught nor take in any sail, but rather hoist every sheet higher than heretofore. So at last they came to the coast of East Gothland.

It was night when Ragnar reached the shore, but wrapped in his garment of tar, and armed with a mighty spear, he set out at once for the house of Herrod the King.

Soon he came to the palace and there beheld a huge monster asleep. Then did Ragnar lift his spear and three times attempt to stab the dragon, but in vain; his spear could not pierce the worm's heavy scales which were as hard as steel. After he had been disturbed for the third time, the monster raised up its huge body and hurled itself at Ragnar, snorting forth fire and venom. It lashed with its tail so that the earth shook all about them. But Ragnar neither trembled nor was afraid at its roaring. As the great dragon coiled itself about, Ragnar perceived an exposed spot under its throat, where the scales were soft, and at this point the hero thrust his spear with all his might. The dragon writhed and turned in agony, so that the great palace trembled, and trees, uprooted, crashed upon the ground. Then suddenly the monstrous worm sank to earth—dead.

The Princess, awakened by the shaking of the palace, crept to her chamber window, terrified. In the darkness below she beheld the victor, in shaggy garments, but ere she could see his visage, he disappeared.

Now as no one could tell what man had killed the monster, King Herrod sent his heralds throughout the land, calling the people together in an assembly in order to find the man who deserved the prize. On the appointed day a great throng gathered without the palace doors. A stranger came among them clothed in shaggy garments covered with tar. The heralds carried about among the people the spear point, taken from the monster's body, in order to find the man whose shaft it fitted. But none of the people possessed a broken spear which matched the point. The haughty heralds passed the stranger by, but he stepped forth, holding a broken weapon which fitted their splintered spear point without flaw. There could be no question that he was the victor.

Herrod looked upon the ragged stranger, amazed and disappointed. "Ha, thou Shaggy-breeches," he exclaimed, "and who taught thee that clever thrust?"

At these words Ragnar dropped his disguise and stood before the assembled people clad in a byrnie* as white as snow, with a gold-rimmed shield hanging before him. His hair was red-gold of hue, falling down in great locks. His shoulders were as broad to look on as the shoulders of two men, and so bright and eager were his eyes that few durst gaze up under the brows of him.

Then the multitude cried as in one voice, "Ragnar, Ragnar, it is King Ragnar himself."

Herrod stepped down from his throne and embraced the hero. Laughing, the King said, "In the future thou shalt be called Shaggy-breeches, in remembrance of this day, and I will give thee the hand of my daughter in marriage."

The King kept his promise, and soon was Ragnar Shaggy-breeches wedded to the Princess Thora. And it is told that each day of the wedding feast was more glorious than the day before it. But ere a month had passed Ragnar brought his fair wife home to Hledra. And there was peace and happiness throughout the North.

* A coat of linked mail.

The Two Brothers and the Forty-Nine Dragons

GREEK

ONCE upon a time there were two brothers. One was very rich and had four children, the other was very poor and had seven children. One day the poor man's wife went to the rich man and said to him, "I am very wretched, for I have not enough bread for my children. I take a little meal and I mix it with a great deal of bran and so manage to make bread. It is well nigh a year since my children have had any relish with their meals; they get nothing but bread and water."

He answered her: "And yet your children are so strong, while mine, with all their feeding and the comforts they enjoy, are always ailing!"

The poor woman said, "God has given us poverty and hunger, but thanks be to Heaven, our children are hale and hearty. Now, therefore, I have come to beg you, if you have any work, not to send for any one but me, so may God send health to your children!" And as she spoke these words, the tears ran from her eyes like a river.

Then he called his wife and said to her:

"Have we any work for her to come and do for us daily, so that she may not sit idle?"

His wife answered him: "Let her come twice a week and knead bread for us."

When she heard these words she was glad, for she thought at once, that when she kneaded that fine white bread they would give her some of it, and her poor children would eat and rejoice. So she rose to go away. And they said to her:

"Goodbye, and remember to come to-morrow morning."

Thus they bade her farewell without giving her a scrap of anything. As she set off home she said to herself, "Would that I were rich, that I might open my cupboard, and bring forth a bit of cheese, or a piece of bread, or at least a little rice, or such like household store to gladden the hearts of the poor!" And lifting her hands to heaven she said: "Why, oh God, hast thou made me so poor?"

And so she went weeping home where her children were waiting for her ever so eagerly, hoping she might bring them something.

But alas, poor thing, she came with empty hands.

The next day she went very early in the morning to the rich man's house to knead bread, and when she had kneaded it and ended her work, they bade her farewell and told her to be sure and come next time, without giving her so much as a cup of cold water.

As soon as she came home the children said to her:

"Have you brought us anything, mother?"

"No!" she said: "may be, when they have done baking they will send us a bit of bread."

But in vain she waited, and when evening came not a loaf nor a plate of anything to eat appeared.

In two or three days they sent word for her to come and knead again, for they liked her kneading much. Then the poor woman arose and went again, and as she was kneading the thought came into her head, not to wash her hands till she got home, and then to wash them in a dish, and to give the wash to her children instead of plain water. So as soon as she had done her kneading, she hurried away, and when she got home she said to her children, "Wait till I give you a little milk soup." And washing her hands well of the dough, she filled a good dish, and gave each one a little to drink.

And they liked it so much that they said, "Mother, whenever you go to knead, mind you bring us some of that broth to drink."

A month passed while she went on at this work. And it seems that God blessed her children, for they grew fatter than ever.

One day as the rich man was passing by the poor man's house, he put his head in at the door and said, "How do you do here?" Then he turns and looks at all the children, and is amazed to see how fat they seem; and going out at the door in a rage, he went home to his wife and called her: "Come here and tell me what you give to my sister-in-law who comes to knead for us."

Now she was frightened at the way he shouted at her and said, "I never gave her anything yet, because I am so afraid of giving her too much and your scolding me."

Says he, "You must have given her something, for her children are so fat they look as if they would burst."

Then she said again, "She takes nothing away with her but her unwashed hands and she washes them at home, and gives the wash to her children to drink."

When he heard that he said, "Put a stop to that, too."

So the next day when the woman went to knead, her mistress waited until she had finished, and when she had done, said to her, "Wash your hands well and then go."

When the poor woman heard that her countenance fell, and she quailed with grief to think how she should go to her children, and they would beg the milk soup of her. When she came to her house her children were gathered together awaiting her, and as soon as they saw her come in they all cried with one voice:

"What have you got, mother?"

"Nothing, children. I forgot myself and washed my hands."

All the children began to weep, and cried, "How could you so forget us, as not to bring us that beautiful broth?"

While they were thus weeping and wailing, the

father entered the house and said, "What ails the children that they cry?"

Then she told him all that had happened, and he was sorely grieved, and made up his mind to kill himself, and so that his wife might not guess his purpose, he asked her for a bag to go to the hill and gather herbs. She gave it him, and he went away. And as he wandered about bewildered for a long while, he found himself at the top of a high crag, and there he made up his mind to fling himself down and die. Then he spied facing the crag a great castle, and he said to himself, "Before I kill myself, I may as well go and see what that castle is like."

And drawing near he saw a tree, and he climbed up into it to see who lived in the castle. After a little while he looked, and behold, a number of dragons came out! He counted them, and they were forty-nine. When the dragons were gone, they left the door open, for that was always their custom. So he climbed down from the tree and went into the castle and walked about it, and saw that it contained much treasure. Then he took his bag and filled it with as much as his back could carry, and went away at once, for he feared lest the dragons should catch him.

When they came back they perceived that a thief had come and stolen some of their money, and from henceforth they determined that one of them should always stay behind in the castle. The poor man returned to the town two days later, and found his wife weeping and refusing to be comforted, for she feared that his affliction had led him to go and kill himself. But when she saw him come back she praised God because he came alive. Then said her husband to her,

"Wife, God has taken pity on our children and on you, who made bread so long at my brother's house, though they never gave you a morsel to feed our little ones. See, here we have enough to live for some time." And opening his bag he showed her the coins.

She was a pious woman, so she said, "The first thing you must buy is some oil that we may light a lamp to our Lady, which we have not done for so long."

And her husband hearkened unto her and straightway went and bought oil, and when they had lighted the lamp they prayed with all their hearts and with tears in their eyes.

The next day her husband arose, and the first thing he did was to buy a house; and he moved into it with his homely furniture and his poor children.

On the first evening he said to his wife, "From day to day we will buy what we want for the house, but nothing more, for we must bear in mind how you used to give milk soup to the children to drink, to save them from dying of hunger."

"Yes," said she, "I will never ask you for anything that we do not want."

Two months passed during which these people lived happily. They did nothing else but go to church and help the poor. One day, then, the wife of the rich man came to visit her poor kinswoman, for she had heard from many that she was now well off, and she herself had begun to suffer misfortune. All her sheep had died, her fields had brought forth no crops, the frost had bitten many of her trees, and she had met with many other mishaps. When the poor woman saw her without being in the least affronted to think how little she had helped her in her own misery, she welcomed her joyfully, and gave her the best seat, and put before her the best things she had to eat in the house; whereas the other, when she went, had only received her in the kitchen, and never asked her to sit down!

After some time, she said, "Sister, pray tell me, where has your husband found work, that my husband may try and find some too, for we have fallen into great distress."

And the poor woman answered her, "My husband has not got any employment, but the day you made me wash my hands he went away—" and then she told her all that had happened.

Then the rich woman asked her to take her husband and show him the dragons. "Perhaps," said she, "we, too, may thus find succor."

And the poor one said to her, "When my husband comes this evening I will tell him, and your husband can go to-morrow, with a bag, along with him."

When the poor man came home at nightfall, his wife told him what had passed, and he said to her,

"I will go and show him the place, but I will not go to gather more treasures for myself, for this which I have God blesses, and it grows from day to day."

Next morning the rich man came with his bag on his back, and said to him, "Good morrow, brother, how do you do? Are you well?" Whereas at other times, if he saw his brother in the way he would turn his back upon him, or take another road, so as not to hear him say that he wanted any help. But when the poor man saw him he got up and kissed him, and said, "Welcome, brother; I daresay it's ten years since I had the happiness of seeing you enter my house."

"Yes," said the rich one, "but now I have fallen into distress, and know not what to do."

Says the poor man, "Let us go; perhaps you will have good luck yet, and get as rich as ever." So they set off for the hill.

And when they got there he showed him the tree, and said to him, "Go aloft and sit in the tree, and soon the dragons will come out. Count them. If there are forty-nine you can come down and enter the castle free from fear; but if, peradventure, they are but forty-eight, do not go in." With these words he went away. In a little while the dragons came out, and he began to count them. But it seems he counted them wrong, and instead of saying forty-eight he said forty-nine. So he came down as fast as he could and went into the castle, and eagerly looked about to see where the treasure was, that he might fill his bag and be gone with all speed, and as he stood there he heard a voice saying, "So you are the thief, and have come back to steal more!" And lo! out comes the dragon which had been watching in a room close by, and seizes him by the head and makes four quarters of him, and hangs them up at the four corners of the dwelling. When the dragons came home, he said to them, "There's no need to keep watch any longer, for I have hung up the four quarters of the thief, and they will guard our castle for us!" And from that day forward they determined, none of them to stay at home, but all of them to go out, and so they began to do.

When two days had passed away the wife of the rich man got restless, and went to the house of her brother-in-law to ask him what they had done with her husband. But the poor man told her what directions he had given him, and said, "I don't know whether he has counted the dragons right, but I will go and see." And off he went. When he came near to the castle, he got up into the tree, and when the dragons came out he counted them with great care, and they were forty-nine in all. Then he came down and went into the castle and looked right and left for his brother. And raising his eyes he looked aloft and beheld his brother hanging in four quarters, and he was sore amazed. Then he lost no time in taking him down, filling his bag with money and going away. When he got home he felt very weary and sad, and said to his wife, "Send some one to my sister-in-law's to tell her to come and take charge of her husband."

And when she came she wept, and would not be comforted on beholding her husband cut into four quarters. Then she said to the poor man, "You must find me a tailor to sew him together, for I cannot bury him like that in four pieces."

The poor man went out at once and got a tailor, who sewed him together. When they had buried and bewailed him, the poor man opened the bag and gave his sister-in-law half the money, and said to her, "Go and get succor for yourself and your children, and if you are in want again, do not blush to come and ask me for what you need." The widow went home with tears in her eyes.

But when the dragons reached their castle and

found the dead man was gone, they all cried aloud, "So the thief has an accomplice!"

The next day, therefore, they went into the town and sought for a tailor to make them forty-nine coats and forty-nine pairs of shoes. So they said to the tailor, "Mind you sew them well so that the stitches don't come out and that they fit us nicely!" And they said it over and over again till the tailor got angry and said to them, "Here's a fuss! why yesterday I had to sew a dead man, who was in four bits, together, and they were quite satisfied with the job, though it was out of my line, and you with your coats are like to craze me!"

Then they said to him, "Pray do you know the man who brought you the dead man to sew?" Said he, "Of course I do, he lives quite close, and if you like I will show you his house, so that you can go and ask him, whether the dead man was well sewed or not."

So he took a dragon with him, and after walking twenty good paces, he showed him the shop. Then the dragons went away to a joiner's, and ordered forty-eight chests, just big enough for them to get into. When they were finished, the forty-eight dragons got inside, and the forty-ninth remained outside. And in the morning the dragon went to the poor man's place, and said to him, "I have had forty-eight chests sent me and I want you to be so kind as to let me leave them here for the night."

"Not for one night only," he answered, "but let them stay as long as you like, and until it suits you to take them away." And he got porters to bring them in.

Then the children of the poor man began to get upon the chests, and jump about, and play on them; and the dragons who were inside, from time to time, groaned and said, "Ah, would it were dark that we might eat them all."

One of the children was playing hide-and-seek with the rest, and he heard these words and these groanings. So he ran to his father and said: "Those chests are bewitched; they are talking."

Then the father thought a moment, and said, "Forty-eight! and the one that brought them makes forty-nine." And he went close up to the chests, and put his ear at the keyhole, and he, too, heard the groaning. So he said to himself, "Now, monsters, I'll make sure of you, now that I have got you in my power."

So off he set at once, and went and bought forty-eight spits, and lighted his kitchen fire, and put them in, and made them red hot, and took them one by one, and thrust them into all the chests. Then he said to his servant: "Look here, my man, they have played us a trick, and put a dragon in a chest, and if we had not killed it, it would have eaten us all up." The servant was angry, and said to his master, "Give it me, and let me go sink it by the seashore?" And he took it on his back, and threw it on to the beach. While he was on his way back, his master made ready another one, and said, "You did not throw it far enough out to sea, and it has come back." And as often as he returned he did the same with all, and threw them into the sea.

But when he got to the last one he grew tired of always coming back and finding one there again, so he walked right into the sea, and plunged it in deep, and when he got back to the shop he called out:

"Master, is it back again?" And his master answered, "No, no, it has not come back. You must have thrown it in very deep." "Aye, master," said he, "I went right into the sea, and plunged it in, and left it."

In the morning the dragon came to see what had become of the chests, and the merchant cunningly told him that one chest was found open. "And I don't know," he added, "what you had inside." The dragon was seized with fear, and went to look at the chests, which were in the back part of the shop. And he found the chest was indeed open, and he trembled. The merchant lost no time, but seized him and flung him into the chest, and made it fast forthwith, and straightway spitted him, and so they were all done for. And the man himself inherited the dragon's castle, and lived there as happy as a prince, and may we live happier still.

The Big Worm

BAHAMAN

ONCE upon a time, in the days when dragons were sometimes called worms, there was a man who had two sons. Now one day the precious fire which they had kept so carefully, feeding it on tender twigs and shoots of trees, went out and only cold black ashes were left.

So the father said to the oldest boy: "See, we have no fire. How can we cook our potatoes without it? We cannot eat them raw, like the animals. Go out, now, and find fire."

So the boy set out and he walked and walked until he saw smoke. Thinking there must be fire he went towards the smoke, but alas! he saw too late that the smoke came from the mouth of a big worm which was full of fire.

The boy approached the creature and said, "Give me some fan (fire)!"

And the worm said, "There is just enough for me. Why should I give you any?"

But the boy said again, "Give me some fire!"

Then the worm said, "Come closer."

So the boy went closer to reach the fire, and the worm swallowed him down at one gulp. The boy went down, down, down inside the worm, until he stopped. There he met many people that the worm had swallowed.

The father and his other son waited a long time for the oldest boy to come back with the fire. When he did not come the father said, "I wonder where my son has gone?"

Then the other boy said, "Father, I'm going to look for him."

So the boy set out, and he walked and he walked a long way until he came to the big worm with the fire in his mouth.

"Give me some fire," said the boy.

"Come and get it," said the worm.

"Give me some fire!" demanded the boy again.

"Time to go home," said the worm. "Come and get fire."

So the boy went closer to get the fire, and the worm swallowed him whole. The boy went down, down, down inside the worm until he met his brother.

Now the boys' father waited a long time for his sons to come home, but they did not come. So finally he said: "My two sons have gone, so I might as well go too, and share their fate."

So the man took down his lance and rubbed it

until it glistened. Sharp it was, too, as only fine steel can be sharp. He set out and traveled a long distance until he came to the big worm.

And the man said to the worm, "Give me some fire."

The worm said: "You're too much for me. I fear your lance. Come and get the fire."

So the man went to get the fire and the worm tried to swallow him. But the man cut and hacked with his lance as he went down inside the worm, and he cut the worm right open. And all the people that the worm had swallowed came walking out, and they built a great city there. And the man found his two sons and they lived in the city ever after.

And this is the end of the story.

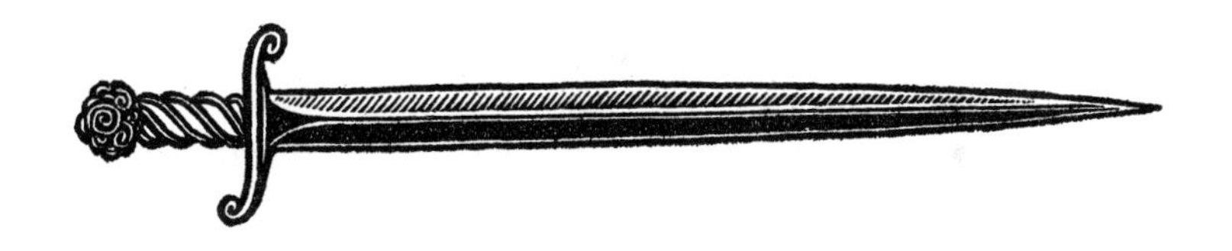

The Story of Lludd and Llevelys

FROM THE MABINOGION

BELI the Great, the son of Manogan, had three sons, Lludd and Caswallawn and Nynyaw; and according to the story he had a fourth son called Llevelys. And after the death of Beli, the kingdom of the Island of Britain fell into the hands of Lludd, his eldest son; and Lludd ruled prosperously, and rebuilt the walls of London, and encompassed it about with numberless towers. And after that he bade the citizens build houses therein, such as no houses in the kingdoms could equal. And moreover he was a mighty warrior, and generous and liberal in giving meat and drink to all that sought them. And though he had many castles and cities, this one loved he more than any. And he dwelt therein most part of the year, and therefore was it called Caer Lludd, and at last Caer London. And after the stranger-race came there, it was called London, or Lwndrys.

Lludd loved Llevelys best of all his brothers, because he was a wise and discreet man. Having heard that the King of France had died, leaving no heir except a daughter, and that he had left all his possessions in her hands, he came to Lludd his brother to beseech his counsel and aid. And that not so much for his own welfare as to seek to add to the glory and honor and dignity of his kindred, if he might go to France to woe the maiden for his wife. And forthwith his brother conferred with him, and this counsel was pleasing unto him.

So he prepared ships and filled them with armed knights, and set forth towards France. And as soon as they had landed, they sent messengers to show the nobles of France the cause of the embassy. And by the joint counsel of the nobles of France and of the princes, the maiden was given to Llevelys, and the crown of the kingdom with her. And thenceforth he ruled the land discreetly and wisely, and happily, as long as his life lasted.

After a space of time had passed, three plagues fell on the Island of Britain, such as none in the islands had ever seen the like of. The first was a certain race that came, and was called the Coranians; and so great was their knowledge, that there was no discourse upon the face of the island, however low it might be spoken, but what, if the wind met it, it was known to them. And through this they could not be injured.

The second plague was a shriek which came on every May-eve over every hearth in the Island of

Britain. And this went through people's hearts, and so scared them that the men lost their hue and their strength, and the young men and the maidens lost their senses, and all the animals and trees, and the earth and the waters were left barren.

The third plague was, that however much of provisions and food might be prepared in the king's courts, were there even so much as a year's provision of meat and drink, none of it could ever be found, except what was consumed in the first night. And two of these plagues no one ever knew their cause, therefore was there better hope of being freed from the first than from the second and third.

And thereupon King Lludd felt great sorrow and care, because that he knew not how he might be freed from these plagues. And he called to him all the nobles of his kingdom, and asked counsel of them what they should do against these afflictions. And by the common counsel of the nobles, Lludd the son of Beli went to Llevelys his brother, King of France, for he was a man great of counsel and wisdom, to seek his advice.

And they made ready a fleet, and that in secret and in silence, lest that race should know the cause of their errand, or any besides the king and his counsellors. And when they were made ready, they went into their ships, Lludd and those whom he chose with him. And they began to cleave the seas towards France.

And when these tidings came to Llevelys, seeing that he knew not the cause of his brother's ships, he came on the other side to meet him, and with him was a fleet vast of size. And when Lludd saw this, he left all the ships out upon the sea except one only; and in that one he came to meet his brother, and he likewise with a single ship came to meet him. And when they were come together, each put his arms about the other's neck, and they welcomed each other with brotherly love.

After that Lludd had shown his brother the cause of his errand, Llevelys said that he himself knew the cause of the coming of those lands. And they took counsel together to discourse on the matter otherwise than thus, in order that the wind might not catch their words, nor the Coranians know what they might say. Then Llevelys caused a long horn to be made of brass, and through this horn they discoursed. But whatsoever words they spoke through this horn, one to the other, neither of them could hear any other but harsh and hostile words. And when Llevelys saw this, and that there was a demon thwarting them and disturbing through this horn, he caused wine to be put therein to wash it. And through the virtue of the wine the demon was driven out of the horn. And when their discourse was unobstructed, Llevelys told his brother that he would give him some insects whereof he should keep some to breed, lest by chance the like affliction might come a second time. And other of these insects he should take and bruise in water. And he assured him that it would have the power to destroy the race of the Coranians. That is to say, that when he came home to his kingdom he should call together all the people, both of his own race and of the race of the Coranians for a conference, as though with the intent of making peace between them; and that when they were all together, he should take this charmed water, and cast it over all alike. And he assured him that the water would poison the race of the Coranians, but that it would not slay or harm those of his own race.

"And the second plague," said he, "that is in thy dominion, behold it is a dragon. And another dragon of a foreign race is fighting with it, and striving to overcome it. And therefore does your dragon make a fearful outcry. And on this wise mayest thou come to know this. After thou hast returned home, cause the island to be measured in its length and breadth; and in the place where thou dost find the exact central point, there cause a pit to be dug, and cause a cauldron full of the best mead that can be made to be put in the pit, with a covering of satin over the face of the cauldron. And then in thine own person do thou remain there watching, and thou wilt see the dragons fighting in the form of terrific animals. And at length they will take the form of dragons in the air. And last of all, after wearying themselves with fierce and furious fighting, they will fall, in the form of two pigs, upon the covering, and they will sink in, and the covering with them, and they will draw it down to the very bottom of the cauldron. And they will drink up the whole of the mead; and after that they will sleep. Thereupon do thou immediately fold the covering around them, and bury them in a kistvaen in the strongest place thou hast in thy dominions, and hide them in the earth. And as long as they shall bide in that strong place, no plague shall come to the Island of Britain from elsewhere.

"The cause of the third plague," said he, "is a

mighty man of magic, who takes thy meat and thy drink and thy store. And he, through illusions and charms, causes everyone to sleep. Therefore it is needful for thee in thy own person to watch thy food and thy provisions. And lest he should overcome thee with sleep, be there a cauldron of cold water by thy side, and when thou art oppressed with sleep, plunge into the cauldron."

Then Lludd returned back unto his land. And immediately he summoned to him the whole of his own race and of the Coranians. And as Llevelys had taught him, he bruised the insects in water, the which he cast over them all together, and forthwith it destroyed the whole tribe of the Coranians, without hurt to any of the Britons.

And some time after this, Lludd caused the island to be measured in its length and in its breadth. And in Oxford he found the central point, and in that place he caused the earth to be dug, and in that pit a cauldron to be set full of the best mead that could be made, and a covering of satin over the face of it. And he himself watched that night. And while he was there, he beheld the dragons fighting. And when they were weary they fell, and came down upon the top of the satin, and drew it with them to the bottom of the cauldron. And when they had drunk the mead they slept. And in their sleep, Lludd folded the covering around them, and in the securest place he had in Snowdon, he hid them in a kistvaen. Now after that this spot was called Dinas Emreis, but before that Dinas Ffaraon. And thus the fierce outcry ceased in his dominions.

And when this was ended, King Lludd caused

an exceeding great banquet to be prepared. And when it was ready, he placed a vessel of cold water by his side, and he in his own proper person watched it. And as he abode thus clad with arms, about the third watch of the night, lo, he heard many surpassing fascinations and various songs. And drowsiness urged him to sleep. Upon this, lest he should be hindered from his purpose and be overcome by sleep, he went often into the water. And at last, behold, a man of vast size, clad in strong, heavy armor, came in, bearing a hamper. And as he was wont, he put all the food and provisions of meat and drink into the hamper, and proceeded to go with it forth. And nothing was ever more wonderful to Lludd, than that the hamper should hold so much.

And thereupon King Lludd went after him, and spoke unto him thus: "Stop, stop," said he, "though thou hast done many insults and much spoil erewhile, thou shalt not do so any more, unless thy skill in arms and thy prowess be greater than mine."

Then he instantly put down the hamper on the floor, and awaited him. And a fierce encounter was between them, so that the glittering fire flew out from their arms. And at the last Lludd grappled with him, and fate bestowed the victory on Lludd. And he threw the plague to the earth. And after he had overcome him by strength and might he besought his mercy.

"How can I grant thee mercy," said the king, "after all the many injuries and wrongs that thou hast done me?"

"All the losses that ever I have caused thee," said he, "I will make thee atonement for, equal to what I have taken. And I will never do the like from this time forth. But thy faithful vassel will I be." And the king accepted this from him.

And thus Lludd freed the Island of Britain from the three plagues. And from thenceforth until the end of his life, in prosperous peace did Lludd the son of Beli rule the Island of Britain. And this tale is called the story of Lludd and Llevelys.

And thus it ends.

The Golden Apple-Tree and the Nine Peahens

SERBIAN

ONCE upon a time there lived a king who had three sons. Now, before the king's palace grew a golden apple-tree, which in one and same night blossomed, bore fruit, and lost all its fruit, though no one could tell who took the apples. One day the king, speaking to his eldest son, said, "I should like to know who takes the fruit from our apple-tree." And the son said, "I will keep guard to-night, and will see who gathers the apples." So when the evening came he went and laid himself down under the apple-tree upon the ground to watch. Just as the apples ripened, however, he fell asleep, and when he awoke in the morning there was not a single one left on the tree. Whereupon he went and told his father what had happened. Then the second son offered to keep watch by the tree, but he had no better success than his eldest brother.

So the turn came to the king's youngest son to keep guard. He made his preparations, brought his bed under the tree, and immediately went to sleep. Before midnight he awoke and looked up at the tree, and saw how the apples ripened, and how the whole palace was lit up by their shining. At that minute nine peahens flew towards the tree, and eight of them settled on its branches, but the ninth alighted near him and turned instantly into a beautiful girl—so beautiful, indeed, that the whole kingdom could not produce one who could in any way compare with her. She stayed, conversing kindly with him, till after midnight, then, thanking him for the golden apples, she prepared to depart; but, as he begged she would leave him one, she gave him two, one for himself and one for the king, his father. Then the girl turned again into a peahen, and flew away with the other eight.

Next morning, the king's son took the two apples to his father, and the king was much pleased, and praised his son. When the evening came, the king's youngest son took his place again under the apple-tree to keep guard over it. He again conversed as he had done the night before with the beautiful girl, and brought to his father, the next morning, two apples as before. But, after he had succeeded so well several nights, his two elder brothers grew envious because he had been able to do what they could not. At length they found an old woman, who promised to discover how the youngest brother had succeeded in saving the two apples. So, as the evening came, the old woman stole softly under the bed which stood under the apple-tree and hid herself. And after a while came also the king's son, and laid himself down as usual to sleep. When it was near midnight the nine peahens flew up as before, and eight of them settled on the branches and the ninth stood by his bed, and turned into a most beautiful girl.

Then the old woman slowly took hold of one of the girl's curls and cut it off, and the girl immediately rose up, changed again into a peahen and flew away, and the other peahens followed her, and so they all disappeared. Then the king's son jumped up, and cried out, "What is that?" and, looking under the bed, he saw the old woman, and drew her out. Next morning he had her severely punished for her deed, but the peahens never came back, and the king's son was very sad for a long time and wept at his loss. At length he resolved to go and look after his peahen, and never to come back again unless he should find her. When he told the king, his father, of his intention, the king begged him not to go away, and said that he would find him another beautiful girl, and that he might choose out of the whole kingdom.

But all the king's persuasions were useless. His son went into the world to search everywhere for his peahen, taking only one servant to serve him. After many travels he came one day to a lake. Now by the lake stood a large and beautiful palace. In the palace lived an old woman as queen, and with the queen lived a girl, her daughter. He said to the old woman, "For heaven's sake, grandmother, do you know anything about nine golden peahens?" And the old woman answered, "Oh, my son, I know all about them; they come every midday to bathe in the lake. But what do you want with them? Let them be, think nothing about them. Here is my daughter. Such a beautiful girl! and such an heiress! All my wealth will remain to you if you marry her." But he, burning with desire to see the peahens, would not listen to what the old woman spoke about her daughter.

Next morning, when day dawned, the prince prepared to go down to the lake to wait for the peahens. Then the old queen bribed the servant and gave him a little pair of bellows, and said, "Do you see these bellows? When you come to the lake you must blow secretly with them behind his neck, and then he will fall asleep, and not be able to speak to the peahens." The mischievous servant did as the old woman told him; when he went with his master down to the lake, he took occasion to blow with the bellows behind his neck, and the poor prince fell asleep just as though he were dead. Shortly after the nine peahens came flying, and eight of them alighted by the lake, but the ninth flew towards him, as he sat on horseback, and caressed him, and tried to awaken him. "Awake, my darling! Awake, my heart! Awake, my soul!" But for all that he knew nothing, just as if he were dead.

After they had bathed, all the peahens flew away together, and after they were gone the prince woke up and said to his servant, "What has happened? Did they not come?" The servant told him they had been there, and that eight of the peahens had bathed, but the ninth had sat by him on his horse, and caressed and tried to awaken him. Then the king's son was so angry that he almost killed himself in his rage.

Next morning he went down again to the shore to wait for the peahens, and rode about a long time till the servant again found an opportunity of blowing with the bellows behind his neck, so that he again fell asleep as though dead. Hardly had he fallen asleep when the nine peahens came flying, and eight of them alighted by the water, but the ninth settled down by the side of his horse and caressed him, and cried out to awaken him, "Arise, my darling! Arise, my heart! Arise, my soul!"

But it was of no use; the prince slept on as if he were dead. Then the ninth peahen said to the servant, "Tell your master to-morrow he can see us here again, but never more." With these words the peahens flew away. Immediately after the king's son woke up, and asked his servant, "Have they not been here?" And the man answered, "Yes, they have been, and say that you can see them again to-morrow, at this place, but after that they will not return again." When the unhappy prince heard that he knew not what to do with himself, and in his great trouble and misery tore the hair from his head.

The third day he went down again to the shore, but, fearing to fall asleep, instead of riding slowly, galloped along the shore. His servant, however, found an opportunity of blowing with the bellows behind his neck, and again the prince fell asleep. A moment after came the nine peahens, and the eight alighted on the lake and the ninth by him, on his horse, and sought to awaken him, caressing him. "Arise, my darling! Arise, my heart! Arise, my soul!" But it was of no use, he slept on as if dead. Then the peahen said to the servant, "When your master awakens, tell him he ought to strike the head of the nail from the lower part, and then he will find me." Thereupon all the peahens flew away. Immediately the king's son awoke, and said to his servant, "Have they been here?" And the servant answered, "They have been, and the one which alighted on your horse ordered me to tell you to strike off the head of the nail from the lower part, and then you will find her." When the prince heard that he drew his sword and cut off his servant's head.

After that he traveled alone about the world, and, after long traveling, came to a mountain and remained all night there with a hermit, whom he asked if he knew anything about nine golden peahens. The hermit said, "Eh, my son, you are lucky; God has led you in the right path. From this place it is only half a day's walk. But you must go straight on, then you will come to a large gate, which you must pass through; and, after that, you must keep always to the right hand, and so you will come to the peahens' city, and there find their palace." So next morning the king's son arose, and prepared to go. He thanked the hermit, and went as he had told him.

After a while he came to the great gate, and, having passed it, turned to the right, so that at midday he saw the city, and beholding how white it shone, rejoiced very much. When he came into the city he found the palace where lived the nine gold peahens. But at the gate he was stopped by the guard, who demanded who he was, and whence he came. After he had answered these questions, the guards went to announce him to the queen. When the queen heard who he was, she came running out to the gate and took him by the hand to lead him into the palace. She was a young and beautiful maiden, and so there was a great rejoicing when, after a few days, he married her and remained there with her.

One day, some time after their marriage, the queen went out to walk, and the king's son remained in the palace. Before going out, however, the queen gave him the keys of twelve cellars, telling him, "You may go down into all the cellars except the twelfth—that you must on no account open, or it will cost you your head." She then went away.

The king's son, whilst remaining in the palace, began to wonder what there could be in the twelfth cellar, and soon commenced opening one cellar after the other. When he came to the twelfth he would not at first open it, but again began to wonder very much why he was forbidden to go into it. "What *can* be in this cellar?" he exclaimed to himself. At last he opened it. In the middle of the cellar lay a big barrel with an open bunghole, but bound fast round with three iron hoops. Out of the barrel came a voice, saying, "For pity's sake, my brother—I am dying with thirst—please give me a cup of water."

Then the king's son took a cup and filled it with water, and emptied it into the barrel. Immediately he had done so one of the hoops burst asunder. Again came the voice from the barrel, "For pity's sake, my brother—I am dying of thirst—please give me a cup of water." The king's son again filled the cup, and took it, and emptied it into the barrel, and instantly another hoop burst asunder. The third time the voice came out of the barrel, "For pity's sake, my brother—I am dying of thirst—please give me a cup of water." The king's son again took the cup and filled it, and poured the water into the barrel, and the third hoop burst. Then the barrel fell to pieces, and a dragon flew out of the cellar, and caught the queen on the road and carried her away.

Then the servant, who went out with the queen, came back quickly, and told the king's son what had happened. The poor prince knew not what to do with himself, so desperate was he, and full of self-reproaches. At length, however, he resolved to set out and travel through the world in search of her. After long journeying, one day he came to a lake, and near it, in a little hole, he saw a little fish jumping about. When the fish saw the king's son, she began to beg pitifully, "Be merciful! Be my brother, and throw me into the water. Some day I may be of use to you, so take now a little scale from me, and when you need me, rub it gently." Then the king's son lifted the little fish from the hole and threw her into the water, after he had taken one small scale, which he wrapped up carefully in a handkerchief.

Some time afterwards, as he traveled about the world, he came upon a fox caught in an iron trap. When the fox saw the prince he spoke: "Be merciful and be a brother to me and help me to get out of this trap. One day you will need me, so take just one hair from my tail, and when you want me, rub it gently." Then the king's son took a hair from the tail of the fox and set him free.

Again, as he crossed a mountain, he found a wolf fast in a trap; and when the wolf saw him it spoke: "Be a brother to me; set me free, and one day I will help you. Only take a hair from me, and when you need me, rub it gently." So he took a hair and set the wolf free.

After that the king's son traveled about a very long time, till one day he met a man to whom he said: "Brother, have you ever heard anyone say where is the palace of the dragon king?" The man gave him very particular directions which way to take, and in what length of time he could get there. Then the king's son thanked him and continued his journey until he came to the city where the dragon lived. When there, he went into the palace and found therein his wife, and both of them were exceedingly pleased to meet each other, and began to take counsel how they could escape. They resolved to run away, and prepared hastily for the journey. When all was ready they mounted on horseback and galloped away.

As soon as they were gone the dragon came home, also on horseback, and, entering his palace, found that the queen had gone away. Then he said to his horse, "What shall we do now? Shall we eat and drink, or go at once after them?" The horse answered, "Let us eat and drink first; we shall catch them anyway; do not be anxious."

After the dragon had dined he mounted his horse, and in a few moments came up with the runaways. Then he took the queen from the king's son and said to him, "Go now! This time I forgive you, because you gave me water in the cellar; but if your life is dear to you do not come back here any more."

The unhappy young prince went on his way a little, but could not long resist his feelings, so he came back next day to the dragon's palace and found the queen sitting alone and weeping. Then they began again to consult how they could get away. And the prince said, "When the dragon comes, ask him where he got that horse, and then you will tell me so that I can look for such another one; perhaps in this way we can escape." He then went away, lest the dragon should come and find him with the queen.

By-and-by the dragon came home, and the queen began to pet him, and speak lovingly to him about many things, till at last she said, "Ah, what a fine horse you have! Where did you get such a splendid horse?" And he answered, "Eh, where I got it every-one cannot get one! Very far from here is a high mountain, where lives an old woman who has twelve horses in her stable, and no one can say which is the finest, they are all so beautiful. But in one corner of the stable stands a horse which looks as if he were leprous, but, in truth, he is the very best horse in the whole world. He is the brother of my horse, and whoever gets him may ride to the sky. But whoever wishes to get a horse from that old woman must serve her three days and three nights. She has a mare with a foal, and whoever during three nights guards and keeps for her this mare and this foal, has a right to claim the best horse from the old woman's stable. But whoever engages to keep watch over the mare and does not, must lose his head."

Next day, when the dragon went out, the king's son came, and the queen told him all she had learned from the dragon. Then the king's son went away to the mountain and found the old woman, and entered her house, greeting her; "God help you, grand-mother!" And she answered, "God help you, too, my son! What do you wish?"

"I should like to serve you," said the king's son.

Then the old woman said, "well, my son, if you keep my mare safe for three days and three nights I will give you the best horse, and you can choose him yourself; but if you do not keep the mare safe you shall lose your head."

Then she led him into the courtyard, where all around stakes were ranged. Each of them had on it a man's head, except one stake which had no head on it and shouted incessantly, "Oh, grandmother, give me a head."

The old woman showed all this to the prince, and said, "Look here, all these were heads of those who tried to keep my mare, and they have lost their heads for their pains."

But the prince was not a bit afraid, so he stayed to serve the old woman. When the evening came he mounted the mare and rode her into the field, and the foal followed. He sat still on her back, having made up his mind not to dismount, that he might be sure of her. But before midnight he slumbered a little, and when he awoke he found himself sitting on a rail and holding the bridle in his hand. Then he was greatly alarmed, and went instantly to look about to find the mare, and while he was looking for her he came to a piece of water. When he saw the water he remembered the little fish, and took the scale from the handkerchief where he kept it and rubbed it a little. Then immediately the little fish appeared and said, "What is the matter, my half-brother?"

And he replied, "The mare of the old woman ran away while under my charge, and now I do not know where she is." And the fish answered, "Here she is, turned to a fish, and the foal to a smaller one. But strike once upon the water with the bridle and cry out 'Heigh! mare of the old woman!' "

The prince did as he was told, and immediately the mare came, with the foal, out of the water to the shore. Then he put the bridle on her and mounted and rode away to the old woman's house and the foal followed. When he got there the old woman gave him his breakfast; she took the mare into the stable, however, and beat her with a poker, saying, "Why did you not go down among the fishes, you cursed mare?" And the mare answered, "I have been down to the fishes, but the fish are his friends, and they told him about me." Then the old woman said, "Then go among the foxes."

When evening came the king's son mounted the mare and rode to the field, and the foal followed the mare. Again he sat on the mare's back until near midnight, when he fell asleep as before. When he awoke, he found himself riding on the rail and holding the bridle in his hand. So he was much frightened, and went to look after the mare. As he went he remembered the words the old woman had said to the mare, and he took from the handkerchief the fox's hair and rubbed it a little between his fingers. All at once the fox stood before him and asked, "What is the matter, half-brother?" And he said, "The old woman's mare has run away, and I do not know where she can be."

Then the fox answered, "Here she is with us; she has turned into a fox, and the foal into a cub; but strike once with the bridle on the earth and cry out, 'Heigh! you old woman's mare!' " So the king's son struck with the bridle on the earth and cried, "Heigh! you old woman's mare!" and the mare came and stood, with her foal, near him. He put on the bridle, and mounted and rode off home, and the foal followed the mare. When he arrived home the old woman gave him his breakfast, but took the mare into the stable and beat her with the poker, crying, "To the foxes, cursed one! to the foxes!" And the mare answered, "I have been with the foxes, but they are his friends, and told him I was there!" Then the old woman cried, "If that is so, you must go among the wolves."

When it grew dark again the king's son mounted the mare and rode out to the field, and the foal galloped by the side of the mare. Again he sat still on the mare's back till about midnight, when he grew very sleepy and fell into a slumber, as on the former evenings, and when he awoke he found himself riding on the rail, holding the bridle in his hand, just as before. Then as before he went in a hurry to look after the mare. As he went he remembered the words the old woman had said to the mare, and he took the wolf's hair from the handkerchief and rubbed it a little. Then the wolf came up to him and asked, "What is the matter, half-brother?" And he answered, "The old woman's mare has run away, and I cannot tell where she is."

The wolf said, "Here she is with us; she has turned herself into a wolf, and the foal into wolf's cub. Strike once with the bridle on the earth and cry out, 'Heigh! old woman's mare!'" And the king's son did so, and instantly the mare came again and stood with the foal beside him. So he bridled her, and galloped home, and the foal followed. When he arrived the old woman gave him his breakfast, but she led the mare into the stable and beat her with the poker, crying, "To the wolves, I said, miserable one." Then the mare answered, "I have been to the wolves; but they are his friends, and told him all about me."

Then the old woman came out of the stable, and the king's son said to her, "Eh, grandmother, I have served you honestly; now give me what you promised me." And the old woman answered, "My son, what is promised must be fulfilled. So look here: here are the twelve horses; choose which you like." And the prince said, "Why should I be too particular? Give me only that leprous horse in the corner; fine horses are not fitting for me." But the old woman tried to persuade him to choose another horse, saying, "How can you be so foolish as to choose that leprous thing while there are such very fine horses here?" But he remained firm by his first choice, and said to the old woman, "You ought to give me which I choose, for so you promised." So when the old woman found she could not make him change his mind, she gave him the leprous-looking horse, and he took leave of her, and went away leading the horse by the halter.

When he came to a forest he curried and rubbed down the horse, and lo! it shone as bright as gold. He then mounted, and the horse flew as quickly as a bird, and in a few seconds brought him to the dragon's palace. The king's son entered and said to the queen, "Get ready as soon as possible." She was soon ready, when they both mounted the horse, and began their journey home.

Soon after the dragon came home, and when he

saw the queen had disappeared, said to his horse, "What shall we do? Shall we eat and drink first, or shall we pursue them at once?" The horse answered, "Whether we eat and drink or not it is all one, we shall never reach them."

When the dragon heard that he got quickly on his horse and galloped after them. When they saw the dragon following them they pushed on quicker, but their horse said, "Do not be afraid; there is no need to run away." In a very few minutes the dragon came near to them, and his horse said to their horse, "Wait a moment, my brother! I shall kill myself running after you." Their horse answered, "Why are you so stupid as to carry that monster? Fling your heels up and throw him off, and come along with me."

When the dragon's horse heard that he shook his head angrily and flung his feet high in the air, so that the dragon fell off and broke in pieces, and his horse came up to them. Then the queen mounted him and returned with the king's son happily to her kingdom, where they reigned together in great prosperity until the day of their death.

The Legend of the Viking's Cave

NORWEGIAN

IN the days of Harald the Fair-Haired, a man named Thorir Oddsson came from Iceland to Norway. He was sent by his uncle Sigmund to a friend of his uncle's named Ulf in the north country.

Thorir spent some time with Ulf, and one night he and his comrades were out fishing and came home late. Ulf came down to the wharf to meet them and as they fastened their boat for the night Thorir saw in the distance a fire like the light of the moon, over which hovered a blue flame.

"Friend Ulf," he said, "what is that light I see yonder on the horizon? Methinks it is as bright as Lady Moon herself. I would know more of it."

Ulf was many years Thorir's senior. "Better not inquire into that," he said, shaking his head solemnly. "That light is of no human origin. Let it alone."

But Thorir persisted. "Why should I not know of it?" he asked. "Even if it be caused by trolls, i' faith, I will learn more."

"That light," said Ulf at length, "is a grave-mound fire." And that was all he would say on the subject.

Still Thorir plied him with questions, and later in the evening as the men sat up over their mead, Ulf yielded to the questions and spoke as follows:

"Once many years ago, before even my grandfather had established his home in this country, there was a berserk (Norse warrior) named Agnar who made this great grave-mound. He hid there a great deal of treasure and went into it with all his ship's crew. Since that time he has guarded the mound by his trolldom so that no one may come near it. Many men there have been who have come to break into it, and they have all died violent deaths or else some great mishap hath befallen them. And even now we do not know whether the troll is alive or dead."

"Now thou hast spoken well," answered Thorir, pleased at obtaining the information. "It is more manly to go after that treasure in the mound than to row out and fish. I shall venture it!"

The men all sprang to their feet at this statement. Thorir towered above them in his great strength as happy as a boy at a new quest.

"Nay, nay, friend Thorir," protested Ulf. "What shall I say to thy uncle when thou dost not return? Peradventure he will think I have urged thee on to this quest." And all the men spoke the same and tried to prevent him from going.

Still Thorir declared he would go. "And is there not one who will go with me?" he asked.

A man named Ketilbjörn stepped out from the group. "I will go," he said quietly. Still Thorir waited and no one else durst volunteer.

Then Thorir clapped Ketilbjörn on the back. "We'll have a try for the treasure," quoth he. "And as for these other faint-hearts—" and he laughed a great laugh that shook the rafters.

Ulf liked it not but he and his men helped fit out Thorir and his good comrade for the quest on the morrow. With the first crack of dawn they were up and away. To reach the mound they had to ascend a hill slope, and as they reached the foot of the hill and started to climb, there broke upon them such a violent storm that they could not stand before it. They had a rope between them and Thorir went on ahead as long as he could, but finally the storm lifted both of them up and threw the two men down the slope. The rope caught around a large stone and both were so exhausted that they lay there until they fell asleep.

As he slept Thorir dreamed a strange dream. He thought that a man came to him, big of body and dressed in a red kirtle, or tunic. On his head was a good helm and he bore aloft a shining sword in his hand. In his broad belt was fixed a good knife and he had gloves on his hands. He was majestic and stately but his countenance was angry.

The man made a thrust at Thorir with the point of his scabbard and spoke to him in an angry tone.

"Wake up, O thou that sleepest!" he said. "Wake up! When thou wilt rob thy kinsmen there is the making of an ill man in thee. But I will do to thee better than thou dost deserve, for I am thy father's brother by the same mother as him. I will give thee presents if thou wilt turn back and look elsewhere for treasure. See, thou shalt have from me this good kirtle, which will shield thee from fire and weapons, and along with it the helm and sword.

"I shall also give thee gloves such as thou wilt never again have the like of, for thy followers will be free from wounds if thou dost stroke their hurts with these gloves. And if thou wilt wear them when thou dost bind up any man's wounds, all the pain will go out of them. Then, too, I shall leave here my knife and belt and these thou shalt always have with thee. And besides all this, I shall give thee twenty marks of gold and twenty of silver."

Thorir pondered all these words thoughtfully. It seemed to him that this was too little from so near and so rich a kinsman.

"I will not go back for any little bribe," he said at length. "Nor did I know that I had trolls so near of kin to me until thou dist tell me. Thou wouldst have no hope of mercy from me were it not for our kinship."

Then Agnar the troll, for it was he, said: "Long will it be ere thy eyes are filled with treasure, and thou mayst well excuse me for loving my wealth for thou wilt love it well too before all is done."

"I care not for thy prophecies of ill," replied Thorir. "I will accept your offer, however, of showing me where I may look for greater treasures if thou dost wish to beg off thy own."

"I will rather do that than quarrel with thee," Agnar said. "Years ago there was a viking named Val, who had much gold which he took into a cave far to the north of here by the sea. He and his sons brooded over the treasure until they were transformed into flying dragons. They have helms on their heads and swords under their arms. I will give thee a cup of which thou shalt drink two draughts and thy comrade one, and then happen whatever may."

So saying the troll disappeared, and Thorir awoke to find all the things Agnar had given him laying beside him. Ketilbjőrn awoke also and as he had heard all their talk and saw where Agnar went he advised Thorir to take this offer. Then Thorir took the cup and drank two draughts of it and Ketilbjőrn one. There was still some liquor left and Thorir set the cup to his mouth again and drank it all. Once more sleep fell on them and Agnar returned and blamed Thorir for having drunk all that was in the cup.

"Because thou hast done this," he said, "thou wilt pay for this drink the latter part of thy life." Agnar also told him many things that befell later and gave him directions how to reach the cave of the viking Val and win the treasure.

After this the two men woke and went home. Thorir told Ulf all that had befallen them and asked the way to Val's cave. Ulf tried again to prevent their going and offered them money to desist, saying that no one who had gone had ever come back.

"Ill it will be for me," he wailed, "should evil befall these men whom my friend Sigmund has sent me. I pray thee do not go."

But Thorir was bent on going at any cost and soon after he and his comrades set out and held north along Finnmark till they came to the fell (mountain) where Val's cave was. A great river fell from the mountain into deep chasms and flowed out into the sea.

Then Thorir knew they had reached the spot to which he was directed, and they all went up on the fell and made the preparations that Agnar had taught him. Thorir had his men cut down a great tree and laid it with its branches hanging over the mountain's edge, piling up stones on its roots. Then they took a cable and fastened it to the branches. Thorir offered his comrades the chance to go and keep all the treasure they got, but none of them had any hope of reaching the cave, even though there were no other danger, and begged him to give up the attempt.

"That shall not be," said Thorir. "Rather will I try myself and have all the treasure that can be found." The other men then said they would make no claim to the treasure.

Thorir threw off his clothes and equipped himself lightly in the kirtle he got from Agnar. He took with him the gloves, belt and knife as well as a slender line that Agnar gave him. He had a javelin that was his father's, and with this he went out on the tree. From the tree he shot the javelin across the river and it caught in the wood on the other side. After that he went down the rope and let the line draw him away under the waterfall. When Ketilbjörn saw this he declared he would go with Thorir and let one fate befall them both. So he too went down the rope, followed by two other men, Thorhall and Thrand.

Thorir had by this time reached the cave, and drew in the other men who had followed him. A rocky projection ran out to the sea in front of the waterfall and up this came Björn and Hyrning, two more of his followers. The tent was beside this projection because no one could stay near the waterfall on account of the tremendous vibration and spray.

Thorir and his men kindled a light in the cave and went on until the wind blew against them and the light went out. Then Thorir called on Agnar for aid and straightway there came a great flash of light from the door of the cave, by which they went on for some way until they heard the breathing of the dragons. As soon as the light came over the dragons they all fell asleep, and then there was no want of light which shone from the dragons and from the gold they lay upon.

On the gold the men saw swords lying with the hilts ready to their hand. Thorir and his comrades seized these at once and then leaped over the dragons and thrust the swords under their shoulders, piercing them to the heart. Thorir took the helm off the largest dragon, but at that moment the monster seized Thrand and flew out of the cave with him. The other dragons followed one by one casting fire and much venom from their mouths. Those who were outside now saw light flashing from the waterfall and ran out of their tent, while the dragons flew up out of the chasm.

Then Björn and the others saw that one of them

had a man in its mouth, and supposed that all who entered the cave must be dead. The biggest dragon who held Thrand flew farthest, and as they came up over the ledge of rock Björn sprang up and thrust his inlaid spear into it. When the dragon received the wound there sprang from it a great quantity of blood into Björn's face, so that he died instantly. The blood and venom fell on the foot of Hyrning causing him such pain that he could scarcely stand.

As for Thorir and his comrades they got great treasure in the cave so that there was sufficient gold and precious things for all the men. They stayed three days in the cave of the viking and there Thorir found the sword, Horn-hilt, that Val had borne in battle. Thorir then climbed up the rope first and afterwards drew up his companions and the treasure.

Thorir stroked Hyrning's foot with the gloves and all the pain left it at once. Then they divided the treasure, Thorir receiving the largest share, and returned to Ulf who rejoiced greatly that they had come back safely.

Years later Thorir was in battle with his enemies and he fled to the northland to the viking's cave. He took with him his two chests which held Val's treasure, and holding them in his arms with a great shout he sprang into the deep chasm. He was never seen again but long afterwards a dragon was seen flying down into the ravine in which he disappeared. The tale is told in the north country that Agnar changed him into a dragon because he drank thrice of the magic mead, and that he broods forever over the viking's treasure.

The Price of Curiosity

AINU

LONG, long ago, in very ancient days, when the world had just been made, there lived a people whom we know to-day as the Ainus, kin to the Japanese.

The world was quite dangerous then, as the crust or covering of the earth was thin, and underneath fires burned, just as to-day there are volcanoes. The poor Ainus had to stay in their little huts, because if they went outside to hunt food the earth might break under their weight and they would fall into the flames that raged beneath the surface.

The Ainus would have starved unless the god Okikurumi had taken care of them. Okikurumi had a kind heart, so every day he went fishing for the Ainus. He usually caught a great many fish, and when he returned home he would give his day's catch to his wife, Turesh, and tell her to go to the Ainus and give them the fish so they would have something to eat. One thing Okikurumi commanded, however, and that was that the Ainus would not attempt to see the face of Turesh, who brought them the fish. He was quite stern when he commanded this, for his wife was very beautiful and he did not want people staring at her.

One day an Ainu grew curious as to this messenger from Okikurumi, and wanted to see what she looked like. So that evening when Turesh came as usual with the fish, this Ainu waited until her hand was stretched in at the window. He seized hold of it and pulled Turesh inside his hut by main force. Poor Turesh struggled and screamed, but to no avail. The Ainu grasped her tightly and there she was.

But even as the Ainu held her, behold! Turesh turned into a wriggling, writhing dragon! Then the sky grew black as night, thunder rolled and lightning flashed, for Okikurumi was very angry at the Ainu who dared lay hands on his wife. A bolt of lightning struck the hut of the wicked Ainu, and in a few minutes it was in flames. The dragon vanished into the air, and Turesh rejoined her husband in her proper form.

The Ainus were sorry for the way one of their tribe had acted, and made offerings and sacrifices to Okikurumi to appease his anger. But the god would not be mollified, and from that day to this he has not fed the Ainus, and they have struggled along as best they could without him. The crust of the earth cooled off, and the Ainus went out and caught fish for themselves, but even though they fished all day they could never catch as much fish or as big fish as they had when Okikurumi sent it to them by his wife, Turesh.

The Story of St. George and the Dragon

Adapted from the Faerie Queen of Edmund Spenser

BY MARY E. CHRISTIE

GLORIANA was the Queen of Fairyland, and her Knights were famed through all the world for valor in fight, for faithfulness in love, and for kindness to the weak. They were ever ready to do battle on the part of any who had suffered wrong, and no pain or labor seemed to them too great to be undergone in such a cause. They worshipped their Queen, who was good, and great, and beautiful, and her favor was the highest reward they coveted. They were called the Knights of Maidenhood.

Now Gloriana held every year a twelve-days' feast, during which it was the custom of the Court that she should grant whatsoever boons were asked of her.

One day, in the beginning of such a feast, a tall clownish young man came before the Queen, and falling at her feet, asked that he might have the achievement of the first adventure that should happen. By this he meant that he should be allowed to undertake the deliverance of the first person who should come to the Fairy Court to ask for help in trouble.

He was a person of no account at Court. None knew whence he came or who he was; he himself was ignorant of his birth and parentage, and he had not as yet borne arms. And such adventures were generally entrusted to knights of renown. But the Queen could not break through the custom of the Court, and she granted him his boon; upon which he sat himself down humbly upon the floor to wait till an adventure should happen, for he knew himself to be too rough in looks and manners to sit among the Knights of the Court.

Soon after there came in a beautiful lady, whose name was Una. She was dressed in white, but over her white dress she wore a black mourning stole. She rode upon a white ass, and behind her came a dwarf leading in one hand a warlike horse, upon the back of which were laid the arms of a knight, and carrying in the other a spear such as was commonly used in battle.

The lady, who appeared very sorrowful, approached Gloriana and told her tale. She was, she said, the daughter of a great King and Queen, who had ruled the most ancient monarchy of the world till a wicked and terrible dragon had laid waste their land and taken them captive; and she implored the Queen to appoint one of her Knights to deliver them.

Thereupon the clownish young man started from the floor and claimed the adventure for himself; at which both the Queen and the lady were displeased, for he seemed to them a most unfit person for so great an exploit, being wholly untried in arms and unpracticed in the ways of courtesy. But he would not forego his desire, and the Queen was mindful of her promise. So in the end the lady was prevailed upon to take him for her Knight, which, however, she consented to do only on the condition that he would wear the armor she had brought with her. To this he was by no means unwilling; and, indeed, when he had dressed himself therein and taken the spear in his hand, it seemed to all present that he was greatly changed, and that now, instead of a clownish person unfit for the service of gentle ladies, he was the goodliest man in all the company.

The Queen laid Knighthood upon him. And as he could not tell what his name was, she called him the Red Cross Knight, because of the blood red cross that was on his breastplate; and sometimes he was called the Knight of Holiness. He mounted upon the warlike horse, and went forth with Una in search of the great dragon whom he was to kill.

So Una and her champion set out together, and the dwarf followed them, carrying provisions necessary for their support, and sometimes he lagged far behind, being tired with his burden. They had to travel a long way, for the country where Una's father and mother were in captivity was very distant from the Court of Gloriana. But Una knew the country and she guided the Knight wisely.

They had time for much talk as they went, and

in the course of it they became very loving friends. For Una was a most sweet lady, full of kindness, and above all of such a pleasant temper that in spite of the great sorrow that was upon her, it seemed to the Knight that wherever she came she brought sunshine with her, even into the most dark and dismal places. And Una found that the Red Cross Knight, far from being the rude person she had thought him in the first moment, was indeed perfected in all the qualities of true knighthood. He was brave and courteous, ever ready to help her in danger, and very gentle and friendly in conversation. For though he had lived far away from Courts and seen little of gentle ladies, his life had been pure and holy, and he had accustomed himself to think with reverence of all that is good and beautiful.

In the middle of their first day's traveling, a heavy storm came on, and they were driven to take shelter in a wood that lay a little apart from the straight way. When the storm was over they could find no way to take them back into the open road. They cast about anxiously for a path, but none opened before them. At last they chanced to meet upon their way an old white-bearded man, of a grave and reverend aspect. His long black gown and bare feet, and the books that hung at his belt, gave him the look of one of those old hermits who used to live apart from the world, and spend all their time in prayer. As he walked, he fixed his eyes on the ground, his lips moved as though he were muttering prayers, and every now and then he knocked his fist against his breast like one who is repenting of his sins.

He saluted the Knight in passing, and the Knight, as was courteous, bowed low to him in answer. And then, drawing the rein of his horse, he asked him if he could tell him news of any adventures happening abroad in the world.

"Ah, my dear son," said the old man, "how should one who lives in a hidden cell, saying his prayers all day, have any tidings to tell of war and worldy trouble? But night is coming on. Come home with me and rest till morning."

The Knight was well content, and they went home to rest in the old man's cell. He had no entertainment to offer them, but they expected none. Rest was all they needed. And after they had sat together a little while talking of saints and saying prayers, darkness came on, and they fell asleep.

Now this old man who had taken the Red Cross Knight and the lady Una into his hut was not at all what he appeared to them. His simple manners and his habit of continually muttering prayers were but an outward show of goodness, put on in order that he might deceive the unwary. He was a great magician, and he called himself Archimago. But his true name was Hypocrisy, and he spent all his life in making things seem other than they were.

As soon as his guests were well asleep, he withdrew to that part of his dwelling where it was his wont to practice his wicked arts. He pored over strange books, and muttered terrible and mighty words, at sound of which bad spirits gathered round him ready to do his bidding. With the help of these he fashioned wicked dreams, and sent them to the sleeping Knight, who was greatly troubled by them.

For Archimago had contrived that in these dreams the lady Una should appear to her Knight with such a living look, and with such close likeness of face and person to her real self, that he should think it was no dream, but awaking truth, and should believe that she was really there.

In these dreams which troubled the Knight, Una behaved in a manner quite unlike herself. She was no longer the modest, simple lady who had won his love as he rode with her in the wood. She was bold in her speech and manner, and said and did things so shocking that the Knight, who thought it all was true, was much perplexed and grieved to the heart. So bitter, indeed, was his anguish at the thought that Una was not the good and true lady he had thought her, that before morning came he rose and mounted his horse and, with the dwarf to keep him company, rode away from the old man's cell without so much as a word of farewell to his lady.

And all the while she, poor soul, had been sleeping innocently, little dreaming what was passing in the mind of her Knight. When morning came she awoke, and rising from her bed went forth to seek him. But in vain. She could not find him anywhere, nor yet the dwarf who hitherto had served her faithfully, waiting upon her every hour of the day. At which, weeping and wailing, she mounted her ass and rode forth to seek them. But the Knight's swift horse had carried him far away, and though Una never rested, but still fared on over hill and dale and wood and plain, she could not overtake him. Very sad and desolate she felt, forsaken so ungently by him whom she loved best. But hardly more sad than the Knight himself, who rode he cared not whither, misled by grief, and wishing only to escape from the sad thoughts that tormented him.

After many wanderings and adventures, Una found her Knight. He, too, had suffered much and knew at last that the dreams he had had of Una were all untrue, and part of a wicked enchantment to separate them. But now they were joined again and they resolved that naught should ever come between them.

Before setting forth again on their quest of the Great Dragon they visited an old hermit who had the gift of much rare knowledge. He could tell many secrets to those who were not too proud to inquire of him, and could show them strange and beautiful sights. To the Red Cross Knight he showed a far-off city on a glistening hill, where he told him that good Knights dwelt forever after they had fought their battles bravely, though in that city, he said, they were called no longer Knights but Saints.

The Red Cross Knight thought this city so passing fair that he was impatient to go to it at once. All his desire for adventure and glory had left him. He longed to be rid of toils and arms, and to rest forever among the Saints.

But the old man said that might not be. "Not yet," he said, "may you desert the royal maid who trusts to your strong arm to slay her father's foe."

"Then," said the Knight, "I will quickly deliver her and come back to this place."

But that was not to be either; the Knight had many battles more to fight before he could go and rest in the fair city.

Before leaving the hut, the Red Cross Knight asked the old man if he could tell him aught of his parentage.

"That I can, truly," answered he. "You are decended from the royal line of Britain's kings, but at your birth you were stolen by a fairy and hidden in the furrow of a field. There a ploughman found you and carried you home and reared you in his cottage, where you remained till your desire for glory drove you to Court to seek for knighthood and adventure. Your name is George, and when your fight is fought, and you are come to the fair city that you see far off, you will be called St. George, and the people of your land will take you for their Patron Saint. St. George of Merry England you will be called, and everywhere your name will be the signal of victory."

The Red Cross Knight was overjoyed at this good promise. He thanked the old man warmly, and then he and Una took up their journey and in a short time arrived within sight of the brazen castle in which the King and Queen were shut up.

Una saw the castle first, and pointed it out to the Knight. "Lo, there," she said, "is the brazen tower in which my dear parents are imprisoned. I think I see them looking from the walls, and see, on the top of the tower the watchman is standing. He is watching for my return and will cry to them that I have come and brought a champion with me."

At that moment they heard a loud roaring sound, and saw the Dragon lying stretched upon the side of the hill on which the castle stood. He rose and hastened towards them. The Knight bade Una stand aside, and went to meet him.

It was well that the Red Cross Knight had not sought the battle sooner, for this was an enemy whom to overthrow would need no common strength and courage. As he came near he seemed a moving mountain, so monstrous was his size. His body was thickly covered with brazen scales; his horrible great knotted tail measured three furlongs long; his wings were like the sails of a great ship; and his stings were sharper than any points of steel. He could run, he could creep, he could fly. It seemed impossible that mortal man could stand against him.

But the Knight was not afraid. He went bravely up and struck at him.

The Dragon flapped his wings, lifted himself suddenly in the air, then darted down again and seized both the Knight and his horse and carried them through the air in his flight. But they were too heavy a burden to be carried long in this way, and he was fain to set them down upon the earth again in a very little while.

The undaunted Knight struck again and again at the Dragon, but his blows made no impression on the scaly armor of the monster, and though he fought all day, when night came there seemed no hope of victory. Faint, weary, sore distressed with heat and toil and wounds, he still fought on. Death would have been welcome, but death would not come.

At last a great blow from the Dragon's tail felled the Knight to the ground, and Una, watching from the hill where she was placed, thought all was over. The great Dragon clapped his wings in sign of victory and laid him down to rest.

Una, full of grief and sorrow, watched the whole

night through. She thought her champion was dead and the battle lost, but she could not leave the spot. All night she watched and prayed and wept.

But lo, next morning, when the sun was rising and she lifted her weary eyes to greet the light, she saw the Knight start up refreshed and strong as a young eagle, ready to renew the fight. For by a most happy chance just where he fell there was a well of wondrous water that had a healing power. And since he had lain in it, all his wounds were gone, his weariness was past, and he was ready to meet his enemy with even greater courage than he had done the day before. Again the fight lasted all through the day, again the evening found the victory uncertain, and the Knight so spent that he could no longer stand against the Dragon's might. Again as the sun went down Una saw her champion overthrown, and thought her cause was lost. Again she watched and wept and prayed through all the weary night.

And again, next morning, as the bright sun shone forth, she looked up and saw the Knight arise, healed and restored, and ready for fresh fight. For lo! just where he fell there flowed a stream of balm from out the Tree of Life, and its waves had cured and rested him.

The Dragon rushed upon him with open jaws, thinking this time to devour him indeed, but the Knight ran his knife boldly through the creature's open mouth, and drove him back. Down fell the monster like a huge rock shattered by a storm. He gasped and groaned, and then his life went forth.

The whole earth shook with his fall, and the Knight himself could not refrain from trembling, so awful was the shock, so long and painful had the fight been.

And as for Una, for awhile she could not believe the victory was really won; but as she saw the Dragon did not move, she gathered courage and ran down and praised and thanked her faithful Knight.

The watchman on the castle-top had seen the two days' fight and now he saw the victory. He ran down and called the news out loudly to the King and Queen, who having made sure that it was true, ordered the brass gates to be thrown open, and came forth to greet their deliverer. A noble company of grave and sober lords went with them, and before them marched a guard of tall young men carrying laurel-branches in sign of peace and victory. They came before the conqueror and laid the laurels at his feet, loudly proclaiming him their patron and their lord. And lovely damsels came with wreaths and timbrels, and danced and sang about Una, and crowned her, half in mirth and half in earnest, as their queen.

The great news spread quickly far and wide, and people flocked from all sides to see and hear. They wondered at the Knight, and thought the lady very fair; but when they saw the Dragon they were frightened, and not believing he was really dead were fain to fly. Little children came near and would have touched him, but their mothers caught them in their arms, and screamed and carried them away.

The King and Queen led the Knight back into their palace, where a great feast was made ready in his honor. Holiday was proclaimed throughout all the kingdom, and all the day passed in rejoicing.

After the feast the King called Una to him, and in the presence of all his court, solemnly betrothed her to the Red Cross Knight.

He said that in the first days of his captivity he had proclaimed that he would give his daughter to whatever champion should slay the Dragon and deliver him and his Queen from bondage, and that most gladly now he gave her to this Knight. And not his daughter only, but his kingdom.

So he prayed the Knight to stay with him and be his heir.

Right glad was Una, and right glad the Knight to hear the King speak so. And, without delay, they clasped hands and vowed to be to one another faithful man and wife.

But all could not be as the King wished, for the Red Cross Knight was bound by the honor of his knighthood to serve the Fairy Queen for six whole years. During that time he must not think of rest, but must wander ceaselessly through Fairyland seeking the Queen's enemies and redressing the wrongs of innocent people.

Una was much grieved to part with him, but she dared not hinder him from his duty. So after he had tarried a little while at her father's court, she let him go with loving farewells and good wishes.

And so St. George went forth upon his six years' service to Queen Gloriana, and Una stayed meanwhile with her father and mother, and waited quietly till the day should come when she and her true Knight could be joyfully wedded, and need part no more.

The Shepherd and the Dragon

BOZENA NEMCOVA

ONCE upon a time there was a shepherd called Baca; when he was tending his sheep it was his duty to live high in the mountains in the herdsman's hut from which he managed everything. When he was herding the sheep it was his habit to whistle with his shepherd's pipe, or to lie on the ground and look up towards the sky and towards the mountains or at the sheep and the green pasture.

One day in the fall, at the time when snakes go into the ground to sleep, the nice shepherd lay on the ground, his head resting on his elbow, looking before him down into the mountain. All of a sudden he saw an astonishing sight: a great multitude of snakes came from all directions to the rock which was before his eyes. When they came to the rock each picked up on his tongue a certain herb which grew there, with this herb he tapped on the rock, it opened and the snakes, one after another, vanished within. Baca got up from the ground, called his dog Dunaj to watch the sheep, then went himself to the rock thinking, "I must find out what the herb is and where the snakes go down." The herb was there; he did not know its kind; but when he plucked it and knocked on the rock with it, the rock opened for him! He went in and saw that he was in a cave whose walls shone with gold and silver. In the center of the cave stood a golden table and on the table coiled in a ring lay a gigantic old serpent. He was asleep. Around the table lay nothing but serpents. All slept, nor did they even stir when the shepherd came in.

Baca liked the cave, as long as it took him to walk around several times, but then the time began to drag and he thought about his sheep and wanted to go back. He thought to himself, "I have seen what I wanted, I will go back." It was easy to say "I will go" but how to do it? The rock had closed behind him when he entered the cave, and what he would have to do, what to say, to make the rock open, the shepherd did not know, and so he had to remain in the cave.

"Oh, well, if I can't get out, I will take a nap," he said finally, and wrapping himself in his sheepskin coat, he lay down on the ground and slept. It did not seem to him that he had slept long when a sort of rustle and murmur disturbed him. He looked around and thought that he was sleeping in the hut; then he awakened a little more, and saw around him the gleaming walls and the golden table; on the table the old serpent, around the table a circle made up of a multitude of serpents. After a while they began to murmur, "Is it time?" The old serpent let them ask, then finally raising his head slowly said, "It is time!" When he had so said, he stretched himself from head to tail like a switch, got down from the table to the ground, and crawled to the entrance of the cave. The snakes all crawled after him.

The shepherd stretched himself deliberately, got up and followed after the serpents, thinking to himself, "When they go out, I will go also." Easy to say "I will go also," but how to do it? The old serpent came to the rock, the rock opened itself, and one after another the snakes went out. When the last snake had gone out the shepherd wanted to go also, but the rock closed before his very nose, and the old serpent said to him in his hissing voice, "Oh, you, fellow, must stay there."

"Oh, what can I do here? You have no farm to work and I cannot sleep forever. Let me go out. I have sheep at the hut and at home a mean wife who will curse me if I do not drive in on time," he begged.

"Never shall you go out of here unless you swear a triple oath never to tell where you were nor how you got in with us," hissed the snake.

What could Baca do? Gladly he bound himself with a triple oath that he would tell nothing, if only he might get outside. "If you are not true to your oath, evil will overtake you," threatened the serpent as he was going out.

How changed it was outside! The shepherd's legs began to shake when he saw how time had passed; that instead of fall, it was spring.

"Misery is mine," he bemoaned himself. "I am

a foolish fellow. What have I done? Actually, I have spent the whole winter in the rock. O my sheep! where have you gone! O my wife, what will you say!" So lamenting bitterly he walked toward the corral. At the corral he saw his wife, and, not ready for her reproaches, he hid himself in the shed. When he sat in the shed, he saw that a fine young gentleman stepped up to his wife from outside and he heard him ask her where her husband was.

The shepherdess burst into tears and told this man how one day in the fall Baca had gone into the forest with his sheep and had never returned. The dog Dunaj took care of the sheep, but as for the shepherd she knew nothing. "Perhaps the wolves tore him to pieces, or the forest women enticed him into the forest," sobbed the woman.

"Oh, don't cry, little wife," called the shepherd then from the shed, "after all I'm alive! The wolves did not tear me, nor did the forest women entice me into the magic forest. I have spent the winter in the shed." But this did not help him any.

When the shepherdess heard his voice, she stopped crying and began to scold him cruelly. "I hope that a hundred thunderbolts will strike your soul, you sluggard, you knave! Aren't you a great fellow? That is a shepherd! He trusts his sheep to the will of God, crawls into the shed and sleeps like a snake in the winter. Who ever heard of such a thing?"

Baca in his heart agreed with his wife, but tell the truth he could not; he must be silent or foresworn. The fine gentleman, however, told the wife to keep still, that her husband did not sleep in the shed, that he must have been somewhere else and that if the shepherd would tell him why he was so silent, he would give him much money. The shepherdess then was all the more angry because her husband had lied to her and she finally demanded to know where he was. No one knows what might have happened, but the fine gentleman promised her money if she kept silent and persuaded her to go home and to let him take care of the shepherd.

When the shepherdess had gone, the fine gentleman changed to his natural form and the shepherd saw before him the wizard of the mountains. He knew him at once because the wizard has in his forehead a third eye. The wizard is a man of great strength, he knows how to change himself into any shape he likes, and if one should try to resist him he would turn him instantly into something else, perhaps a sheep.

The shepherd was very much afraid of the wizard; he had for him even greater respect than for his wife.

The wizard asked him where he was and what he saw. Baca was dreadfully afraid of this question. What should he tell? He was afraid of the old serpent and a broken oath and he was afraid also of the three-eyed wizard. But when the wizard asked him for a second time, for the third, and then asked him again with an angry voice where he was and what he saw, when the wizard seemed to grow larger and larger before his very eyes, he forgot his oath. He told him where he was and what he saw in the rock and how he got in.

"That's good," said the wizard, "come with me, show me your rock and your herb." Baca had to go.

When they came to the rock, the shepherd picked the herb, knocked on the rock, and the rock opened.

The wizard did not want Baca to enter nor did he himself go farther; he drew out some kind of book and began to read from it. The shepherd turned pale with fright. Then all at once the earth began to tremble, from the rock there sounded hissing and whistling, and out came a fearful dragon, into which the old snake had changed himself. His head was monstrous, from his mouth he breathed out fire, with his tail he lashed to the right and to the left and whenever he hit a tree, it was slashed off.

"Put this bridle on his neck," said the wizard, giving Baca a set of reins, but without taking his eyes from his book. Baca took the reins but was afraid to come near the dragon. Then when the wizard spoke to him a second and a third time, he had to obey. And then woe to poor Baca! As he was aiming to throw the reins about his neck, the dragon turned towards him, and before Baca knew what was happening, he was seated on the dragon's back, and the dragon was flying with him over the forest.

At once it was pitch dark, except for the fire which flashed from the eyes and mouth of the dragon and lighted their journey. The earth quaked, rocks fell down from the peaks. Angrily the dragon lashed his sides, blowing down the pine trees as he went along, snapping them off like twigs, and pouring water down upon the earth until it seemed to run down from the mountains, like the river Vah. It was a horror of horrors. Baca was half dead.

After a while the dragon became a little quieter; he lashed about him less violently, he stopped throwing down water, and flames ceased to flash from his eyes. Baca came to himself, and thought that the dragon was going down. But it was not enough; the dragon acted as if he wished to punish him still further. Little by little, he rose higher and higher above the mountains, ever higher, until the very highest peaks seemed to Baca like ant-hills; and ever higher mounted the dragon until poor Baca could see nothing but the sun, stars and clouds, and the dragon seemed to hang with him along in the air.

"Oh God, what can I do! I am hanging in the air! If I jump down, it will kill me, and I cannot jump up into the heavens!" so Baca cried and began to weep bitterly. The dragon did nothing. "O dragon, O powerful lord dragon, have pity!" he begged the dragon after a while. "Go down farther, I swear to God that I will not anger you again as long as I live."

Baca's plea was enough to melt a stone but the dragon puffed and snorted and said nothing, nor did he move. Then from a distance came to the ears of Baca the voice of a lark. Baca rejoiced. Nearer and nearer to him came the lark; when he was close to him Baca said, "O little lark, bird of the dear God, I beg you, fly to the Father in Heaven and tell him my wretchedness. Tell him that I send him greetings and I call for the help of God."

The lark flew to the Father in Heaven and delivered Baca's message. The Father in Heaven had pity on Baca, wrote something in gold letters on a birch leaf, put the leaf in the lark's beak, and told her to drop it on the dragon's head. The lark flew through the air and flying over the dragon's head, dropped on it the birch leaf with the gold writing. In a twinkling the dragon with Baca dropped to the earth.

When Baca came to his senses he saw that he was in his cottage at the clearing; he saw how the dog Dunaj guarded the sheep and on the window he saw a little bell,

and no more tale have I to tell.

The Legend of Drachenfels

GERMAN

AROUND the castled crag of Drachenfels hang many legends, but the one of which story-tellers spun tales and ancient bards sang in vast halls is that of Siegfried the Great, Lord of the Nibelungen.

The Nibelungen were a warlike people who had grown into a powerful kingdom and whose lands were vast and flourishing. At the time Arthur of Britain held his famous court and Round Table, Siegmond was King of the Nibelungen, and in the city of Xanten near Cleves, now in Holland, was born Siegfried the Horned, his celebrated son.

Siegfried grew fast into stalwart young manhood, becoming indeed almost a giant for he was the incarnation of human strength and power. As he came to man's estate it was natural that he should search for a fair and beautiful woman to wed. So one morning in summer Siegfried, Lord of the Nibelungen, set forth in state from his father Siegmond's home. Already the bards had sung his praises in hymns and every one had done him honor. His fame had spread over the land so wherever he went the name of Siegfried was known.

And now with twelve true knights he set forth to strange lands, for his heart impelled him to far Burgundy where lived Chriemhilda the Fair, daughter of a great king. So joyous was he at the sight of the Rhine that he and his knights hailed the Seven Mountains which towered over them with shouts of exaltation.

"Ho, my companions," called Siegfried. "Let us now renew our ancient troth with Childerich. See, there is his palace yonder, wreathed with grapevines. The very flowers of this beautiful place send their fragrance to welcome us. Many a kindly speech hath my sire sent to him, so of a surety he will keep us within his halls until the morrow be spent."

With one accord the little company turned to the palace of the king, but as they approached the castle they noted that no brilliant torches burned outside, and no snatch of song from a happy people greeted them. Solitude seemed to sit among the towers, and along the silent courts the wind moaned as if telling of a great sorrow that could not otherwise be spoken. A fear fell upon the knights and only Siegfried's courage kept them on their way.

Slowly they passed through the gates and unchallenged made their way into the court. Far down the vast hall was the king, seated on his great throne, his head bowed on his hands in wordless grief.

Around him sat his courtiers silent as stone. At the sound of the cavalcade the king looked up and slowly came down from his throne to greet Siegfried and make him welcome. His trembling arms encircled the bold young hero in kindly clasp, as he looked at the son of his staunch friend through the long grey locks which hung over his eyes. Sorrow and age had bowed the king and Siegfried's heart bled for the old man.

"I greet thee, potent prince," said Siegfried, as he in turn clasped the old man's arm. "How comes this cloud of grief that sits upon your brow? You are the exalted ruler of the Franks, truly one of the bravest peoples in all the country. You have their plighted troth. What more may mortal crave?"

"Alas!" the old king answered, sighing gustily. "Why do I live? If only I could lie down in peace in the grave."

"Yet once on a time, O king," returned Siegfried, "the voice of song echoed through these halls. The praises of thy fair daughter were echoed to the rafters. Where now doth Gunhilda braid her golden hair? So rare a maiden is a sight to look upon, and many years have passed since as children we looked upon each other."

Held speechless with grief the old king lifted his trembling hand and pointed to Drachenfels. "Alas, and woe is me," he sighed, as his tears fell. "No more my darling daughter dwells here. All is over! She lies deep in a cavern in yon rude rock's breast, held in chains by magic power. The tale is sad."

"Oh, tell it," cried Siegfried, and all stood at attention while the old king spoke.

"Sir Hunold, Lord of Drachenfels, whose towers touch yonder skies," said the king, "had wooed my child, Gunhilda, many a year. So fierce he was and black of countenance that my sweet dove shrank from him and loved him not. He vowed to plot her ruin for she would not have him, and by the powers of magic which he wields he lured her to yon cavern and chained her to a rock. Then he took upon himself the semblance of a dragon and watches her day and night. Oh, spawn of hell," the old king shouted, distracted at the thought, "would he were dead and hacked into a thousand pieces. He has overthrown full fifty knights who have tried to rescue her. Whoever saves her, to him shall I give half my kingdom and my throne!"

Siegfried listened with growing wrath at such a tale of woe and horror. Then he said: "I fear not to meet that dragon. Weep not, O king, and comfort thyself. I'll bring thy daughter back to thy arms."

The king clasped the Lord of the Nibelungen to his heart. The young man's courage and bravery gave him renewed strength and once more the king's soul was glad and his glance full of fire.

"My Siegfried," he cried, "most noble youth, if on this earth there lives the one to slay that fiend it is indeed thee. Thou, and thou alone, art the one and thy coming hither shall be blessed forever. The prize is not to be scorned: share my throne, look deep into my daughter's eyes, and one hundred of my noblest steeds laden with my richest treasure—all this shall be for thee."

But Siegfried with a wave of his hand and

friendly word brushed aside the noble offer. Quick at the king's signal the bards and musicians rose to send out sweet strains into the night. Round the festal board went the goblets of heavy gold, full to the brim of Rhine wine that gladdens the hearts of men. High on the king's seat at his side sat Siegfried and long they feasted and drank to the deeds of the morrow. And later still Siegfried slept on downy couch for well he knew that he would need all his strength with the dawn.

When day had climbed the rosy heights of the Seven Mountains Siegfried was ready, clad in all his noble armor. His steed, the strong Grani, swift as the wind, the best that ever a warrior's stable bred, awaited his master's touch on the bridle. One leap and Siegfried was mounted and away. Up, up the mountain side he sped until the towers of Cologne the holy city were glimpsed in the distance. Dimly in the west he saw the morning star keeping faithful watch over the world. Soft breezes blew through the thick foliage. It was a morning when the world seemed fresh from its creator's hands, and not a day to hold such strange and dark adventure.

Yet Siegfried kept sternly to his quest. Holding his lance in rest he drew near the dark cavern where dwelt fear and death. Undaunted he paused before the mouth of the den and shouted, "Monster, come forth!"

The cave resounded with echoes that leaped from point to point and mocked him faintly in response. Then a giant hissing was heard and with horrid shrieks the monster bounded out of the cavern. It was a sight to chill the stoutest heart. The dragon's very look seemed almost powerful enough to kill the brave hero. Quickly Siegfried leaped aside for such a sight was indeed terrible. The monster's eyes sparkled like coals from hell, and noxious vapors arose from his throat. His tail seemed coiled in a thousand knots and when he roared the valleys and plains echoed in afright. He shrieked and tore at the trembling ground and all around him the woods and rocks groaned in chorus.

A lion's mane rose along his murky brown neck, and his jaws gaped like a portcullis swung wide. His terrible fangs seemed like swords, while his fearful claws were great hooks to rend the brave knight who challenged him.

Breathing a prayer to heaven Siegfried charged the monster and then began a fearful battle the like of which has never been seen before or since. Suddenly his lance snapped! All seemed lost for his strength was ebbing too. He sprang aside, dodging the gaping jaws, and with a quick gesture snatched his trusty sword Balmung, that bright blade he won with the Nibelungen treasure, the best sword ever forged. Nothing mortal could behold that shining sword and the dragon shrank back at the sight of it. As he retreated Siegfried pressed on, and then within the cavern he saw the fair Gunhilda. She clasped her white hands to heaven, imploring help for her rescuer.

Stern in his stirrups stood Siegfried, dashing on toward the monster. Bright over his head his sword Balmung flamed and flashed as he brought it down with all the force of a thunderbolt. The whole weight of the hero's body was behind that stroke and it crashed full on the dragon's crest. The roar of ten thousand bulls was not louder than the monster's cry, and lo! before the sun had fully risen the fight was over.

With the going out of the dark soul of Hunold the enchantment on the maiden Gunhilda melted into nothing. The chains fell from off her beauteous arms and she was free to leave the cavern. Timidly she came forth as though she feared the light of day and held out her hand to her deliverer. Mute and amazed Siegfried stood.

The fair Gunhilda was in a shining white robe and her long hair fell around her shoulders in waves of yellow light. Twin tears of pearl stood in her soft blue eyes, as when at dawn the dew sparkles on a violet. Although at first she sighed sadly, soon she smiled and looked joyously on the Lord of the Nibelungen.

"Soon shalt thou see thy sire!" Siegfried promised, as he gently swung the blushing maid upon his steed. Together they hastened down the mountain but already the old king was on his way to meet them. He toiled laboriously up the steep side of the crag and with a shout of joy he hailed his lost Gunhilda. He clasped her fondly in his arms and father and daughter were reunited.

Over and over again the king tried to thank Siegfried but the words would not come. Great tears rolled down his cheeks as he led his daughter and her savior back to the castle for a feast to celebrate her rescue.

Siegfried marveled at the beauty of the fair Gunhilda and when she besought him to tarry longer at their court he longed to do so. But he was on his way to sue for the hand of the beauteous Chriemhilda of the Burgundian court, and to hesitate would have seemed unworthy of him.

Sadly Gunhilda saw him on his way and just as sadly the Lord of the Nibelungen exchanged love, honor and friends for the sword thrusts of future foes. He turned his back on the verdant shores of the Rhine little knowing he would never see them again. Better far had he remained among the loyal Franks, wooing the fair Gunhilda. Perhaps then he would not have fallen by the traitor's spear. But destiny bade him go and the hero journeyed on to wider fields and greater deeds.

Yanni and the Dragon

THESSALIAN

ONCE in the days when the world was much younger than it is now, there lived in the province of Thessaly in ancient Greece, a happy-go-lucky youth named Yanni.

Now this youth was in love with a fair maiden called Yannáki, and love had smiled on him and prospered his suit. The maiden's father had agreed to the match, and Yanni's step was light as he turned homeward on this warm summer evening, for in five days he would be married to his dear love.

So happy was he as he walked home in the moonlight that Yanni sang aloud and laughed with joy. He had nothing to worry him, for he had a fruitful farm, and many cattle and sheep. Life was beautiful, and he caroled forth his joy in song. The nightingale heard him and sang back, for all the world loves a lover and wishes him well.

But there was one who had no love for the sweet voice of Yanni, and who was angry at being aroused from sleep. Among the rocks that rose high above the road were a dragon and his mate, and they were wroth at the youth who had dared waken them. A great roar broke the beauty of the night, and Yanni trembled and turned to fly before it was too late.

But across the path came the dragon, roaring as he came. "Who was it singing who woke me from my sleep, and turned slumber from the eyelids of my mate? I shall eat him for my supper. Where is he?"

Then the dragon spied Yanni who knelt in supplication before the monster.

"Oh, spare me, gentle dragon," pleaded Yanni. "Let me live but five days longer. Next Sunday is my wedding-day, and on Monday is the great wedding-feast. And on Tuesday morn I must take my bride home. If thou wilt spare me until then I promise thee on my honor to return hither and let thou do with me as thou wilt."

By this time the moon had shivered under a cloud at the dragon's roaring, but the morning star, bright and glorious, shone fearlessly out in the sky.

"Who art thou, youth?" asked the dragon, quite wide awake by now and willing to listen to argument.

Then Yanni stood erect and determined within himself to overcome the dragon by courage.

"I am the Lightning's son," he said boldly. "And as thou knowst, Lightning is the daughter of Thunder, so Thunder is my grandfather. If thou wilt not let me depart in peace, Thunder will visit thee and Lightning shall utterly destroy thee."

The dragon pondered this brave speech, and noted the kingly bearing of the youth who stood before him.

"Nay, Yanni," the monster said at length, "I will not harm thee. Thou mayst depart now and need never return unto me. But see that when next thou pass this way that thy voice be still and hushed, else I will destroy thee. Go, and good luck to thee, and may good fortune follow thee and they wife forever!"

So Yanni returned to his home, and the following Sunday was married amid much rejoicing. After the great wedding-feast he brought his fair bride, Yannáki, to their home, but by another way than that which the dragon claimed.

The Dragons of Lucerne

SWISS

SOME five hundred years ago, in the city of Lucerne high up in the Swiss Alps, there lived an honest cooper. He worked hard at his trade, and sang merrily all day long as he earned bread for his little family. He was contented with life and had not a care in the world, but it kept him busy from morn till night earning enough to keep his six children in shoes and clothes, and to buy food for their healthy young stomachs.

His wife was an industrious woman, and together they managed to keep the wolf from the door and present a good appearance to their neighbors. The cooper loved to lock up his little shop at the close of day and hurry down the road to his small house, where there was always a savory soup waiting for him on the table, and perhaps, if times were good, a bit of meat. On this particular night the children greeted him with shouts of joy, and his wife bestirred herself to put the supper on the table.

It was a chill evening in early autumn, and after supper the children crept closer to the fire as the wind howled outside, and the rain fell steadily on the roof. Each morning as the cooper went to his shop he looked across at the majestic shape of Mount Pilatus, that mighty mountain guarding the boundaries of Lucerne and Unterwald. This mountain is the most famous of all the peaks in the beautiful Swiss Alps, and even in those days many legends clung about it.

"Mother," begged thc oldest boy, as he sat idly whittling a stick near the fire, "tell us the story of Mount Pilatus and how it got its name."

"Yes, yes," begged the other children; so the mother settled down to her knitting and told the story she had often told before, while the cooper looked on with a pleased smile at the happy group. While the rain fell and the wind whistled around the house, the mother told the legend of Pontius Pilate, who, when banished by the Roman Emperor Tiberius from Italy, wandered over the mountains to Mount Pilatus, and threw himself into a black lake at the summit of the mountain. On stormy nights, so the oldest inhabitants say to this day, his shadowy form wanders the mountain paths, as he bewails his sin in the judgment hall of long ago.

"And does he still wash his hands, mother?" asked the younger brother eagerly, well knowing the answer.

"Yes," said the mother, "he washes his hands over

and over again. He can never get them clean. And once a year he appears clad in his official robes, and anyone who is unlucky enough to see him then will die before the year is out.

"But that is only a story," she said briskly, in a more cheerful tone. "The real name of Mount Pilatus was first *Mons Fractus,* or, as we would say, the Broken Mountain, because there are great jagged rocks on top of it. But I believe, with the rest of our people, that it was called *Mons Pileatus* first, because that means the capped mountain."

"Why is it capped?" asked the younger brother, dreamily. He objected to having his story spoiled.

"Because of the clouds that gather around it, son," answered his mother. "When you go outdoors every morning you always look up at Mount Pilatus, don't you? So do the rest of us who live here in Lucerne. We can then tell what the weather will be all day, or at least we are warned not to wander too far if Pilatus is thickly covered with clouds. You know the rhyme we have."

The children did know it, and said it together, vying with each other gleefully to see who could shout it the loudest.

> If Pilatus wears his cap, serene will be the day;
> If his collar he puts on, you may venture on the way;
> But if his sword he wields, at home you'd better stay!

"Sh! sh!" said the mother warningly. "You'll wake up the baby. If you know that so well, how many of you can tell me how our lake got its name?"

They all knew that, too. Long ago, when the clank of Roman armor was heard in Alpine fastnesses, a lighthouse shone out across Lake Lucerne, and from it—*lucerna*—both town and lake took their names.

But when the cooper started for his work the next morning his good wife looked up at Mount Pilatus as usual, and she did not like what she saw. The mountain indeed was a weather prophet to the people who lived within sight of it, for all the storms of that region centered around its crest.

"Pilatus has more than his cap and collar on this morning," said the cooper. "I must gather some wood to-day, but the mist reaches far down the mountain. He wields his sword for certain to-day."

"Wait until to-morrow to go for the wood," his wife begged. "I am afraid if you go this morning you will be caught in a storm."

To allay her fears the cooper said he would wait until the next day to go after the wood he needed, but later in the morning he found he had come to the end of his supply. He needed staves for the barrels he was making, and the only way to get it was to climb the steep sides of Mount Pilatus and gather some wood. So forgetting his promise to his wife, he started out to climb the mountain.

After spending several hours in the forest the cooper had gathered quite a lot of wood, and he prepared to go back home. He suddenly realized he had lost his way and while trying to find the path again his foot slipped on a rock and he fell into a deep ravine. He was unhurt, although he had fallen a considerable distance, and he tried to climb up the sides of the gully. The descent was so sheer and precipitous that try as he would he could not secure a foothold. After several attempts he realized it was useless, so he began to walk along the bottom of the ravine, hoping to find a way out.

After a time he came to the mouth of a cavern in the rocks. Pausing a moment, he looked in and then entered boldly. He came out into an open space, like a great room, with high arched ceilings from which hung dripping stalactites, the whole being lighted with an odd flickering light that seemed to come from some fire. As his eyes grew accustomed to the twilight the cooper saw to his horror two huge, fire-breathing dragons. It was the flame from their nostrils which lighted the cave.

The poor cooper gave himself up for lost, and crossed himself again and again. He sank on his knees and offered up a prayer to heaven for his protection. His piety and humble demeanor made an impression on the dragons, so that they closed their huge jaws, which were all ready to devour him, and instead, like Daniel's lions, fawned on him and licked his hands like great dogs.

The cooper gradually forgot his fears and began to pet the monsters, and to feel quite kindly toward them. They shared their food with him, which proved to be a stream flowing from the rocks. The cooper found it had a salty taste but was singularly pleasant, and when he had drunk of it he had no further desire for food. He then lay down and slept all night.

The next day he awoke to the same grey light in the cavern and thought he would explore his new shelter. He found there was no other entrance to the cave, and that it was only the one big room where the dragons slept. He left the cave and went back up the ravine, trying in every way possible to find an escape from the sad situation fate had placed him in. He had no inclination to stay longer with the dragons, in spite of their seeming gentleness. He feared they might change their attitude toward him and snap him up as an after-dinner tidbit.

After several days of exploring the cooper was forced to conclude there was no escape. He would have sunk into desperate melancholy save for his belief that as long as he could keep alive there must be some way of escape. He continued to drink of the magic stream and found he needed no other food.

Thus six months went by, and the poor man's family mourned him as dead.

"He must have perished in that storm on Mount Pilatus," they all said, with sad shakings of their heads, and his sorrowful wife felt he had gone from her forever.

One day spring came suddenly, and the cooper felt new energy and a glad feeling that something must happen to rescue him. That morning the two dragons woke to life and activity. They had slept as snug and safe as bears in their den during the winter, but something now called to them from the outdoors. Slowly they wormed their way out of the cavern into the ravine. They stretched and shook themselves carefully, shaking each wing and paw to be sure they were in good condition. Then to the amazement of the man who was watching them intently one of the dragons suddenly rose in the air, flew in ever-widening circles above him, and then swept majestically out of sight.

Slowly the second dragon started to follow its

mate, but the cooper came to life. With a desperate leap he grasped the monster by the tail and clung to it like a drowning man to a log. Up, up, up into the blue rose the dragon, with each sweep gaining new zest and life. And to its tail clung the cooper, praying to all the saints for his safe deliverance.

When the dragon was over the outskirts of Lucerne, the beast began to descend slowly. Within a short distance of the earth the monster flicked his tail and the cooper was forced to let go. Down, down, down he sank on to the soft deep grass where he lay like one dead. People passing by had seen the astonishing sight and came over to him.

"Is he dead, perchance?" they asked one another in hushed voices, for it was not every day that a dragon descended from the sky and dropped a human being on to the ground.

"Nay, not so," said another. "Look, he moves!"

The cooper sat up and cried out in bewilderment. He told his name and trade, and learned he was a little way from his native city. A crowd had gathered and word of his wonderful experience flew from mouth to mouth. Soon he was united with his wife and children, and there was great rejoicing.

Being a devout man the cooper gave a beautiful communion service to the Church of St. Leodegarius of Lucerne, as a thank-offering for his escape from the dragons, and his preservation while in their cave. He had engraved on the silver service, as a lasting memorial to his rescue, a quaint picture of himself and the dragons in their cave on Mount Pilatus.

The Young Dragon

JULIA BROWN

HE was a very handsome young dragon; at least, so thought his fond parents. He was covered with glittering scales which on his body and wings shaded from blue to green like a peacock's breast. They were golden on his feet and the tips of his wings, while his head glowed like a ruby, his little emerald eyes deep set in it. The effect as he flew about in the sunshine was quite gorgeous.

He lived with his father and mother in the heart of a mountain, the entrance to which was a cave in the side.

Now the young dragon's father was one of the most influential members of the community and the prominent dragons often gathered in his home to talk over the questions of the age. Their most engrossing topic was:

"What shall be our attitude toward man?"

The Conservative dragons contended that it should be entirely external (the dragon outside of the man), but the young dragon's father, who was the head of the Liberal party, said this was all wrong.

In olden times, he conceded, when knights went about with the avowed intention of slaying dragons, such sentiments were natural (not that he wondered at the knights when dragons so far forgot themselves as to carry off young and edible princesses), but, in these enlightened times, there should be peace between the races. Dragons could be useful to men and, possibly, men might even be of use to dragons.

At this, the members of the Conservative party smiled, derisively.

There were occasions when the discussions grew so heated that the flames poured from the dragons' nostrils. These came out at the top of the mountain and caused the people living near to observe, anxiously:

"The volcano seems very active to-night. I fear we may look for an eruption soon."

The young dragon had been carefully trained by his parents to look upon man as a friend, and was even taught his speech. One evening, as he was strolling along in the forest, he walked, with the heedlessness of the young, into a trap. It had not been set for him, but for the Killiowhacs which infested the mountain side. He struggled to escape, but only succeeded in tangling himself more firmly in the ropes of green withes at the bottom of the trap. Here he hung all night, in the most painful position. Early in the morning, however, he perceived a horseman approaching and immediately closed his left eye. This rendered him invisible and he had no wish to frighten the steed of the traveler. Then he accosted him, thus:

"Kind sir, will you be good enough to come to the assistance of a struggling creature?"

The horseman started and looked about him. Seeing no one he asked:

"Who speaks to me?"

"I," said the young dragon. "If you will but tie your horse a little way off, out of sight, I will become visible."

The youth, full of curiosity to discover from whence came the mysterious voice, complied with its request, then advanced toward the trap.

The young dragon opened his left eye and the traveler stopped, suddenly.

"Nay," quoth the dragon, "fear nothing. You see I am quite helpless and in great pain. If you will take your sword and cut the withes I shall be most grateful." Seeing the youth still hesitated, he continued:

"I will not only be grateful, but will hold myself bound, on the honor of a dragon, to do you service."

The stranger hesitated no longer, but, advancing to the trap, cut with his sharp sword the snare which bound the dragon. As he drew himself painfully out, the young dragon said:

"I am unutterably thankful to you, noble sir. May I ask to whom I owe my life and my freedom?"

"I am Prince Yotun, ruler of this country," replied his deliverer. The young dragon bowed low as he responded:

"Now my service and, indeed, my life are yours, should you need them, to the end of my years, and that is no short term. What is your Royal Highness's age?"

"Twenty years," answered the Prince.

"Ah," remarked the dragon, "I am over eighty, but that is very young, as we dragons usually live to a thousand years. Take this scale," he continued, detaching one from his back, "and whenever you need my services present it at the cave in yonder mountain side."

"The fire mountain?" said the Prince.

"Oh, do you call it that?" said the young dragon, smiling. The Prince drew back a little; dragons smile very broadly.

After a few more words the Prince mounted his steed and rode away, while the young dragon, whose wings were too bruised to use, limped painfully to his home. Once arrived there, his mother bound up his wounds with an ointment made from the marrow of the Ichthyosaurus, after a recipe which had been in her family for aeons, and in a few days he was well again.

It was some time after this that, as the young dragon sat at the mouth of the cave, he saw approaching a horse and rider, and thoughtfully closed his left eye. A nearer view, however, caused him to exclaim:

"The Prince!" and hasten toward him. In his surprise he opened his eye, whereupon the horse reared in terror. The Prince controlled him and the dragon immediately became invisible, apologizing for his thoughtlessness.

"How can I serve your Royal Highness?" he

inquired. The Prince, who was looking haggard and wan, replied:

"My betrothed, the Princess Uralia, has been abducted by the giant Borumgum and carried off to his castle. I am now on my way to rescue her and came to ask if you could render me any assistance."

"Certainly," said the young dragon, "I am proud to do so. If your Highness will remain here I will run and fetch her."

"Oh, no!" exclaimed the Prince, "I cannot consent to that. I must myself hasten to her relief at once."

"Oh, very well," said the young dragon, "you go on and I will meet you there." Saying which, he spread his wings and flew away to the giant's castle.

Arrived there he circled around until he espied, at a window in a high tower, a maiden pale with weeping. He flew close to her and said:

"Excuse me, but is this the Princess Uralia?"

The Princess was much surprised at the voice, which apparently came from the air, as the dragon was invisible, but she answered:

"It is indeed the unfortunate Princess Uralia, in the power of that detestable giant Borumgum. But who speaks to me?"

"A friend of the Prince Yotun, who is bound to do him service for service rendered."

"Oh," exclaimed the Princess, who was a quick-witted little thing, "you must be the dragon whose life he saved. You may open your left eye, I shall not be alarmed."

"Now that is sensible," thought the young

dragon, as he complied. The sun was shining upon his brilliant scales and the Princess exclaimed:

"What lovely colors you are! I am glad to have seen you." The young dragon was much flattered.

"Get upon my back," said he, moving close to the window, "and I will return you to your father's palace." The Princess obeyed and they started.

In the meantime the Prince Yotun had arrived at the castle gates. He tethered his steed outside and, creeping through a crack, entered the great courtyard where he found the giant Borumgum (who was fifty feet high) standing in front of his door. Advancing toward him the Prince exclaimed, loudly:

"Wretch, instantly restore to me my betrothed, the beautiful Princess Uralia!"

"Eh?" said the giant, surprised, looking all around him.

"Release the Princess Uralia, at once!" shouted the Prince. Here the giant discovered him and, smiling good-naturedly, said:

"Oh, it's you, is it? Now what do you want?" and, to bring himself a little nearer to the level of the Prince, he sat down upon his doorstep. Once more the Prince angrily repeated his demand for the release of the Princess, but the giant shook his head.

"Couldn't think of it," he said, "she is a very beautiful Princess and I want her to look at. I believe," he added, thoughtfully, "I shall keep her for a mantel ornament."

This made the Prince furious and he drew his sword and slashed at the giant's foot.

"Ouch!" roared the giant as he jumped up, "see here, youngster, don't you know it's rude to stick pins into people?" and he went into his castle in high dudgeon and banged the door after him.

It was useless for the Prince to think of opening it, but while he was debating what to do next, he heard a voice saying:

"If your Highness will climb up on my back I will take you to the palace," and there was the young dragon with the Princess Uralia.

The Prince joyfully embraced his betrothed, then, creeping out through the crack of the great gate, he untied his steed and turned his head toward home, knowing the good horse could be trusted to find his way to the royal stables. Then he mounted the dragon's back, and as they flew toward the palace of the Princess she told him of her capture by the giant Borumgum and her rescue by the young dragon.

"After I have seen you safely home," said the dragon, "I will collect some of my Conservative friends and we will return and dispose of the giant. He is really getting to be a nuisance."

Arrived at her home, both Princess and Prince lavished thanks upon him, but the young dragon, complacently twirling his moustache, said:

"Do not mention it, your Royal Highnesses. It was really a very little thing, for me."

"At least," said the Princess, unfastening from her neck a long and massive golden chain, "at least, I must beg you to accept this slight token of my gratitude," and she clasped it about his throat.

Blushing with pleasure (and when a red-headed dragon blushes he turns a beautiful heliotrope), the young dragon said he would wear the chain all his life. And he did, although, of course, when he shut his left eye it did not affect the gift of the Princess, and people were often much surprised to see a heavy golden chain floating through mid-air.

The next day the wedding of Prince Yotun and Princess Uralia was celebrated with great splendor in her father's palace, the young dragon (with his left eye closed) looking on from one of the open windows.

That evening, as he sat alone in front of the cave, he said to himself:

"My father and mother were right; human beings are very interesting and agreeable and—" here the young dragon sighed, gently—"and fascinating."

He was thinking of the Princess.

The Last of the Dragons

E. NESBIT

OF course you know that dragons were once as common as motorbuses are now, and almost as dangerous. But as every well-brought-up prince was expected to kill a dragon and rescue a princess, the dragons grew fewer and fewer, till it was often quite hard for a princess to find a dragon to be rescued from. And at last there were no more dragons in France and no more dragons in Germany, or Spain, or Italy, or Russia. There were some left in China, and are still, but they are cold and bronzy, and there never were any, of course, in America. But the last real live dragon left was in England, and of course that was a very long time ago, before what you call English History began. This dragon lived in Cornwall in the big caves amidst the rocks, and a very fine big dragon, quite seventy feet long from the tip of its fearful snout to the end of its terrible tail. It breathed fire and smoke, and rattled when it walked, because its scales were made of iron. Its wings were like half-umbrellas—or like bat's wings, only several thousand times bigger. Everyone was very frightened of it, and well they might be.

Now the King of Cornwall had one daughter, and when she was sixteen, of course, she would have to go and face the dragon. Such tales are always told in royal nurseries at twilight, so the Princess knew what she had to expect. The dragon would not eat her, of course—because the prince would come and rescue her. But the Princess could not help thinking it would be much pleasanter to have nothing to do with the dragon at all—not even to be rescued from him.

"All the princes I know are such very silly little boys," she told her father. "Why must I be rescued by a prince?"

"It's always done, my dear," said the King, taking his crown off and putting it on the grass, for they were alone in the garden, and even kings must unbend sometimes.

"Father, darling," said the Princess presently, when she had made a daisy chain and put it on the King's head, where the crown ought to have been. "Father, darling, couldn't we tie up one of the silly little princes for the dragon to look at—and then I could go and kill the dragon and rescue the Prince? I fence much better than any of the princes we know."

"What an unladylike idea!" said the King, and put his crown on again, for he saw the Prime Minister coming with a basket of new-laid Bills for him to sign. "Dismiss the thought, my child. I rescued your mother from a dragon, and you don't want to set yourself up above her, I should hope?"

"But this is the *last* dragon. It is different from all other dragons."

"How?" asked the King.

"Because he *is* the last," said the Princess, and went off to her fencing lesson, with which she took great pains. She took great pains with all her lessons—for she could not give up the idea of fighting the dragon. She took such pains that she became the strongest and boldest and most skilful and most sensible princess in Europe. She had always been the prettiest and nicest.

And the days and years went on, till at last the day came which was the day before the Princess was to be rescued from the dragon. The prince who was to do this deed of valor was a pale prince, with large eyes and a head full of mathematics and philosophy, but he had unfortunately neglected his fencing lessons. He was to stay the night at the palace, and there was a banquet.

After supper the Princess sent her pet parrot to the Prince with a note. It said:

"Please, Prince, come on to the terrace. I want to talk to you without anybody else hearing.—The Princess."

So, of course, he went—and he saw her gown of silver a long way off shining among the shadows of the trees like water in starlight. And when he came quite close to her he said:

"Princess, at your service," and bent his cloth-of-gold-covered knee and put his hand on his cloth-of-gold-covered heart.

"Do you think," said the Princess earnestly, "that you will be able to kill the dragon?"

"I will kill the dragon," said the Prince firmly, "or perish in the attempt."

"It's no use your perishing," said the Princess.

"It's the least I can do," said the Prince.

"What I'm afraid of is that it'll be the most you can do," said the Princess.

"It's the only thing I can do," said he, "unless I kill the dragon."

"Why you should do anything for me is what I can't see," said she.

"But I want to," he said. "You must know that I love you better than anything in the world."

When he said that he looked so kind that the Princess began to like him a little.

"Look here," she said, "no one else will go out to-morrow. You know they tie me to a rock, and leave me—and then everybody scurries home and puts up the shutters and keeps them shut till you ride through the town in triumph shouting that you've killed the dragon, and I ride on the horse behind you weeping for joy."

"I've heard that that is how it is done," said he.

"Well, do you love me well enough to come very quickly and set me free—and we'll fight the dragon together?"

"It wouldn't be safe for you."

"Much safer for both of us for me to be free, with a sword in my hand, than tied up and helpless. *Do* agree."

He could refuse her nothing. So he agreed. And next day everything happened as she had said.

When he had cut the cords that tied her to the rocks they stood on the lonely mountain side looking at each other.

"It seems to me," said the Prince, "that this ceremony could have been arranged without the dragon."

"Yes," said the Princess, "but since it has been arranged with the dragon——"

"It seems such a pity to kill the dragon—the last in the world," said the Prince.

"Well, then, don't let's," said the Princess; "let's tame it not to eat princesses but to eat out of their hands. They say everything can be tamed by kindness."

"Taming by kindness means giving them things to eat," said the Prince. "Have you got anything to eat?"

She hadn't, but the Prince owned that he had a few biscuits. "Breakfast was so very early," said he, "and I thought you might have felt faint after the fight."

"How clever," said the Princess, and they took a biscuit in each hand. And they looked here and they looked there, but never a dragon could they see.

"But here's its trail," said the Prince, and pointed to where the rock was scarred and scratched so as to make a track leading to the mouth of a dark cave. It was like cart ruts in a Sussex road, mixed with the marks of sea gulls' feet on the sea sand. "Look, that's where it's dragged its brass tail and planted its steel claws."

"Don't let's think how hard its tail and its claws are," said the Princess, "or I shall begin to be frightened—and I know you can't tame anything, even by kindness, if you're frightened of it. Come on. Now or never."

She caught the Prince's hand in hers and they ran along the path towards the dark mouth of the cave. But they did not run into it. It really was so very *dark*.

So they stood outside, and the Prince shouted: "What ho! Dragon there! What ho within!" And from the cave they heard an answering voice and great clattering and creaking. It sounded as though a rather large cotton mill were stretching itself and waking up out of its sleep.

The Prince and the Princess trembled, but they stood firm.

"Dragon—I say, Dragon!" said the Princess, "do come out and talk to us. We've brought you a present."

"Oh, yes—I know your presents," growled the dragon in a huge rumbling voice. "One of those precious princesses, I suppose? And I've got to come out and fight for her. Well, I tell you straight, I'm not going to do it. A fair fight I wouldn't say no to—a fair fight and no favor—but one of these put-up fights where you've got to lose— No. So I tell you. If I wanted a princess I'd come and take her, in my own time—but I don't. What do you suppose I'd do with her, if I'd got her?"

"Eat her, wouldn't you?" said the Princess in a voice that trembled a little.

"Eat a fiddle-stick end," said the dragon very rudely. "I wouldn't touch the horrid thing."

The Princess's voice grew firmer.

"Do you like biscuits?" she asked.

"No," growled the Dragon.

"Not the nice little expensive ones with sugar on the top?"

"No," growled the dragon.

"Then what *do* you like?" asked the Prince.

"You go away and don't bother me," growled the dragon, and they could hear it turn over, and the clang and clatter of its turning echoed in the cave like the sound of the steam hammers in the arsenal at Woolwich.

The Prince and Princess looked at each other. What *were* they to do? Of course it was no use going home and telling the King that the dragon didn't want princesses—because His Majesty was very old-fashioned and would never have believed that a new-fashioned dragon could ever be at all different from an old-fashioned dragon. They could not go into the cave and kill the dragon. Indeed, unless he attacked the Princess it did not seem fair to kill him at all.

"He must like something," whispered the Princess, and she called out in a voice as sweet as honey and sugar-cane:

"Dragon! Dragon, dear!"

"WHAT?" shouted the dragon. "Say that again!" and they could hear the dragon coming towards them through the darkness of the cave. The Princess shivered, and said in a very small voice:

"Dragon—Dragon, dear!"

And then the dragon came out. The Prince

drew his sword and the Princess drew hers—the beautiful silver-handled one that the Prince had brought in his motor-car. But they did not attack; they moved slowly back as the dragon came out, all the the vast scaly length of him, and lay along the rock—his great wings half spread and his silvery sheen gleaming like diamonds in the sun. At last they could retreat no farther—the dark rock behind them stopped their way—and with their backs to the rock they stood swords in hand and waited.

The dragon drew nearer and nearer—and now they could see that he was not breathing fire and smoke as they had expected—he came crawling slowly towards them wriggling a little as a puppy does when it wants to play and isn't quite sure whether you're not cross with it.

And then they saw that great tears were coursing down its brazen cheeks.

"Whatever's the matter?" said the Prince.

"Nobody," sobbed the dragon, "ever called me 'dear' before!"

"Don't cry, dragon dear," said the Princess. "We'll call you 'dear' as often as you like. We want to tame you."

"I *am* tame," said the dragon—"that's just it. That's what nobody but you has ever found out. I'm so tame that I'd eat out of your hands."

"Eat what, dragon dear?" said the Princess. "Not biscuits?"

The dragon slowly shook its heavy head.

"Not biscuits?" said the Princess tenderly. "What, then, dragon dear?"

"Your kindness quite undragons me," it said.

"No one has ever asked any of us what we like to eat—always offering us princesses, and then rescuing them—and never once, 'What'll you take to drink the King's health in?' Cruel hard I call it," and it wept again.

"But what would you like to drink our health in?" said the Prince. "We're going to be married to-day, aren't we, Princess?"

She said that she supposed so.

"What'll I take to drink your health in?" asked the dragon. "Ah, you're something like a gentleman, you are, sir. I don't mind if I do, sir. I'll be proud to drink your and your good lady's health in a tiddy drop of"—its voice faltered—"to think of you asking me so friendly like," it said. "Yes, sir, just a tiddy drop of puppuppuppuppupetrol—tha—that's what does a dragon good, sir——"

"I've lots in the car," said the Prince, and was off down the mountain like a flash. He was a good judge of character, and he knew that with this dragon the Princess would be safe.

"If I might make so bold," said the dragon, "while the gentleman's away—p'raps just to pass the time you'd be so kind as to call me 'Dear' again, and if you'd shake claws with a poor old dragon that's never been anybody's enemy but his own—well, the last of the dragons'll be the proudest dragon there's ever been since the first of them."

It held out an enormous paw, and the great steel hooks that were its claws closed over the Princess's hand as softly as the claws of the Himalayan bear will close over the bit of bun you hand it through the bars at the Zoo.

And so the Prince and Princess went back to the palace in triumph, the dragon following them like a pet dog. And all through the wedding festivities no one drank more earnestly to the happiness of the bride and bridegroom than the Princess's pet dragon, whom she had at once named Fido.

And when the happy pair were settled in their own kingdom, Fido came to them and begged to be allowed to make himself useful.

"There must be some little thing I can do," he said, rattling his wings and stretching his claws. "My wings and claws and so on ought to be turned to some account—to say nothing of my grateful heart."

So the Prince had a special saddle or howdah made for him—very long it was—like the tops of many tramcars fitted together. One hundred and fifty seats were fitted to this, and the dragon, whose greatest pleasure was now to give pleasure to others, delighted in taking parties of children to the seaside. It flew through the air quite easily with its hundred and fifty little passengers, and would lie on the sand patiently waiting till they were ready to return. The children were very fond of it and used to call it Dear, a word which never failed to bring tears of affection and gratitude to its eyes. So it lived, useful and respected, till quite the other day—when some one happened to say, in his hearing, that dragons were out of date, now so much new machinery had come. This so distressed him that he asked the King to change him into something less old-fashioned, and the kindly monarch at once changed him into a mechanical contrivance. The dragon, indeed, became the first airplane.

A CATALOG OF SELECTED

DOVER BOOKS

IN ALL FIELDS OF INTEREST

A CATALOG OF SELECTED DOVER BOOKS IN ALL FIELDS OF INTEREST

THE CLARINET AND CLARINET PLAYING, David Pino. Lively, comprehensive work features suggestions about technique, musicianship, and musical interpretation, as well as guidelines for teaching, making your own reeds, and preparing for public performance. Includes an intriguing look at clarinet history. "A godsend," *The Clarinet,* Journal of the International Clarinet Society. Appendixes. 7 illus. 320pp. 5⅜ x 8½. 40270-3

HOLLYWOOD GLAMOR PORTRAITS, John Kobal (ed.). 145 photos from 1926-49. Harlow, Gable, Bogart, Bacall; 94 stars in all. Full background on photographers, technical aspects. 160pp. 8⅜ x 11¼. 23352-9

THE ANNOTATED CASEY AT THE BAT: A Collection of Ballads about the Mighty Casey/Third, Revised Edition, Martin Gardner (ed.). Amusing sequels and parodies of one of America's best-loved poems: Casey's Revenge, Why Casey Whiffed, Casey's Sister at the Bat, others. 256pp. 5⅜ x 8½. 28598-7

THE RAVEN AND OTHER FAVORITE POEMS, Edgar Allan Poe. Over 40 of the author's most memorable poems: "The Bells," "Ulalume," "Israfel," "To Helen," "The Conqueror Worm," "Eldorado," "Annabel Lee," many more. Alphabetic lists of titles and first lines. 64pp. 5³⁄₁₆ x 8¼. 26685-0

PERSONAL MEMOIRS OF U. S. GRANT, Ulysses Simpson Grant. Intelligent, deeply moving firsthand account of Civil War campaigns, considered by many the finest military memoirs ever written. Includes letters, historic photographs, maps and more. 528pp. 6⅛ x 9¼. 28587-1

ANCIENT EGYPTIAN MATERIALS AND INDUSTRIES, A. Lucas and J. Harris. Fascinating, comprehensive, thoroughly documented text describes this ancient civilization's vast resources and the processes that incorporated them in daily life, including the use of animal products, building materials, cosmetics, perfumes and incense, fibers, glazed ware, glass and its manufacture, materials used in the mummification process, and much more. 544pp. 6⅛ x 9¼. (Available in U.S. only.) 40446-3

RUSSIAN STORIES/RUSSKIE RASSKAZY: A Dual-Language Book, edited by Gleb Struve. Twelve tales by such masters as Chekhov, Tolstoy, Dostoevsky, Pushkin, others. Excellent word-for-word English translations on facing pages, plus teaching and study aids, Russian/English vocabulary, biographical/critical introductions, more. 416pp. 5⅜ x 8½. 26244-8

PHILADELPHIA THEN AND NOW: 60 Sites Photographed in the Past and Present, Kenneth Finkel and Susan Oyama. Rare photographs of City Hall, Logan Square, Independence Hall, Betsy Ross House, other landmarks juxtaposed with contemporary views. Captures changing face of historic city. Introduction. Captions. 128pp. 8¼ x 11. 25790-8

AIA ARCHITECTURAL GUIDE TO NASSAU AND SUFFOLK COUNTIES, LONG ISLAND, The American Institute of Architects, Long Island Chapter, and the Society for the Preservation of Long Island Antiquities. Comprehensive, well-researched and generously illustrated volume brings to life over three centuries of Long Island's great architectural heritage. More than 240 photographs with authoritative, extensively detailed captions. 176pp. 8¼ x 11. 26946-9

NORTH AMERICAN INDIAN LIFE: Customs and Traditions of 23 Tribes, Elsie Clews Parsons (ed.). 27 fictionalized essays by noted anthropologists examine religion, customs, government, additional facets of life among the Winnebago, Crow, Zuni, Eskimo, other tribes. 480pp. 6⅛ x 9¼. 27377-6

FRANK LLOYD WRIGHT'S DANA HOUSE, Donald Hoffmann. Pictorial essay of residential masterpiece with over 160 interior and exterior photos, plans, elevations, sketches and studies. 128pp. 9¼ x 10¾. 29120-0

THE MALE AND FEMALE FIGURE IN MOTION: 60 Classic Photographic Sequences, Eadweard Muybridge. 60 true-action photographs of men and women walking, running, climbing, bending, turning, etc., reproduced from rare 19th-century masterpiece. vi + 121pp. 9 x 12. 24745-7

1001 QUESTIONS ANSWERED ABOUT THE SEASHORE, N. J. Berrill and Jacquelyn Berrill. Queries answered about dolphins, sea snails, sponges, starfish, fishes, shore birds, many others. Covers appearance, breeding, growth, feeding, much more. 305pp. 5¼ x 8¼. 23366-9

ATTRACTING BIRDS TO YOUR YARD, William J. Weber. Easy-to-follow guide offers advice on how to attract the greatest diversity of birds: birdhouses, feeders, water and waterers, much more. 96pp. 5³⁄₁₆ x 8¼. 28927-3

MEDICINAL AND OTHER USES OF NORTH AMERICAN PLANTS: A Historical Survey with Special Reference to the Eastern Indian Tribes, Charlotte Erichsen-Brown. Chronological historical citations document 500 years of usage of plants, trees, shrubs native to eastern Canada, northeastern U.S. Also complete identifying information. 343 illustrations. 544pp. 6½ x 9¼. 25951-X

STORYBOOK MAZES, Dave Phillips. 23 stories and mazes on two-page spreads: Wizard of Oz, Treasure Island, Robin Hood, etc. Solutions. 64pp. 8¼ x 11. 23628-5

AMERICAN NEGRO SONGS: 230 Folk Songs and Spirituals, Religious and Secular, John W. Work. This authoritative study traces the African influences of songs sung and played by black Americans at work, in church, and as entertainment. The author discusses the lyric significance of such songs as "Swing Low, Sweet Chariot," "John Henry," and others and offers the words and music for 230 songs. Bibliography. Index of Song Titles. 272pp. 6½ x 9¼. 40271-1

MOVIE-STAR PORTRAITS OF THE FORTIES, John Kobal (ed.). 163 glamor, studio photos of 106 stars of the 1940s: Rita Hayworth, Ava Gardner, Marlon Brando, Clark Gable, many more. 176pp. 8⅜ x 11¼. 23546-7

BENCHLEY LOST AND FOUND, Robert Benchley. Finest humor from early 30s, about pet peeves, child psychologists, post office and others. Mostly unavailable elsewhere. 73 illustrations by Peter Arno and others. 183pp. 5⅜ x 8½. 22410-4

YEKL and THE IMPORTED BRIDEGROOM AND OTHER STORIES OF YIDDISH NEW YORK, Abraham Cahan. Film Hester Street based on *Yekl* (1896). Novel, other stories among first about Jewish immigrants on N.Y.'s East Side. 240pp. 5⅜ x 8½. 22427-9

SELECTED POEMS, Walt Whitman. Generous sampling from *Leaves of Grass*. Twenty-four poems include "I Hear America Singing," "Song of the Open Road," "I Sing the Body Electric," "When Lilacs Last in the Dooryard Bloom'd," "O Captain! My Captain!"–all reprinted from an authoritative edition. Lists of titles and first lines. 128pp. 5³⁄₁₆ x 8¼. 26878-0

THE BEST TALES OF HOFFMANN, E. T. A. Hoffmann. 10 of Hoffmann's most important stories: "Nutcracker and the King of Mice," "The Golden Flowerpot," etc. 458pp. 5⅜ x 8½. 21793-0

FROM FETISH TO GOD IN ANCIENT EGYPT, E. A. Wallis Budge. Rich detailed survey of Egyptian conception of "God" and gods, magic, cult of animals, Osiris, more. Also, superb English translations of hymns and legends. 240 illustrations. 545pp. 5⅜ x 8½. 25803-3

FRENCH STORIES/CONTES FRANÇAIS: A Dual-Language Book, Wallace Fowlie. Ten stories by French masters, Voltaire to Camus: "Micromegas" by Voltaire; "The Atheist's Mass" by Balzac; "Minuet" by de Maupassant; "The Guest" by Camus, six more. Excellent English translations on facing pages. Also French-English vocabulary list, exercises, more. 352pp. 5⅜ x 8½. 26443-2

CHICAGO AT THE TURN OF THE CENTURY IN PHOTOGRAPHS: 122 Historic Views from the Collections of the Chicago Historical Society, Larry A. Viskochil. Rare large-format prints offer detailed views of City Hall, State Street, the Loop, Hull House, Union Station, many other landmarks, circa 1904-1913. Introduction. Captions. Maps. 144pp. 9⅜ x 12¼. 24656-6

OLD BROOKLYN IN EARLY PHOTOGRAPHS, 1865-1929, William Lee Younger. Luna Park, Gravesend race track, construction of Grand Army Plaza, moving of Hotel Brighton, etc. 157 previously unpublished photographs. 165pp. 8⅞ x 11¾. 23587-4

THE MYTHS OF THE NORTH AMERICAN INDIANS, Lewis Spence. Rich anthology of the myths and legends of the Algonquins, Iroquois, Pawnees and Sioux, prefaced by an extensive historical and ethnological commentary. 36 illustrations. 480pp. 5⅜ x 8½. 25967-6

AN ENCYCLOPEDIA OF BATTLES: Accounts of Over 1,560 Battles from 1479 B.C. to the Present, David Eggenberger. Essential details of every major battle in recorded history from the first battle of Megiddo in 1479 B.C. to Grenada in 1984. List of Battle Maps. New Appendix covering the years 1967-1984. Index. 99 illustrations. 544pp. 6½ x 9¼. 24913-1

SAILING ALONE AROUND THE WORLD, Captain Joshua Slocum. First man to sail around the world, alone, in small boat. One of great feats of seamanship told in delightful manner. 67 illustrations. 294pp. 5⅜ x 8½. 20326-3

ANARCHISM AND OTHER ESSAYS, Emma Goldman. Powerful, penetrating, prophetic essays on direct action, role of minorities, prison reform, puritan hypocrisy, violence, etc. 271pp. 5⅜ x 8½. 22484-8

MYTHS OF THE HINDUS AND BUDDHISTS, Ananda K. Coomaraswamy and Sister Nivedita. Great stories of the epics; deeds of Krishna, Shiva, taken from puranas, Vedas, folk tales; etc. 32 illustrations. 400pp. 5⅜ x 8½. 21759-0

THE TRAUMA OF BIRTH, Otto Rank. Rank's controversial thesis that anxiety neurosis is caused by profound psychological trauma which occurs at birth. 256pp. 5⅜ x 8½. 27974-X

A THEOLOGICO-POLITICAL TREATISE, Benedict Spinoza. Also contains unfinished Political Treatise. Great classic on religious liberty, theory of government on common consent. R. Elwes translation. Total of 421pp. 5⅜ x 8½. 20249-6

MY BONDAGE AND MY FREEDOM, Frederick Douglass. Born a slave, Douglass became outspoken force in antislavery movement. The best of Douglass' autobiographies. Graphic description of slave life. 464pp. 5⅜ x 8½. 22457-0

FOLLOWING THE EQUATOR: A Journey Around the World, Mark Twain. Fascinating humorous account of 1897 voyage to Hawaii, Australia, India, New Zealand, etc. Ironic, bemused reports on peoples, customs, climate, flora and fauna, politics, much more. 197 illustrations. 720pp. 5⅜ x 8½. 26113-1

THE PEOPLE CALLED SHAKERS, Edward D. Andrews. Definitive study of Shakers: origins, beliefs, practices, dances, social organization, furniture and crafts, etc. 33 illustrations. 351pp. 5⅜ x 8½. 21081-2

THE MYTHS OF GREECE AND ROME, H. A. Guerber. A classic of mythology, generously illustrated, long prized for its simple, graphic, accurate retelling of the principal myths of Greece and Rome, and for its commentary on their origins and significance. With 64 illustrations by Michelangelo, Raphael, Titian, Rubens, Canova, Bernini and others. 480pp. 5⅜ x 8½. 27584-1

PSYCHOLOGY OF MUSIC, Carl E. Seashore. Classic work discusses music as a medium from psychological viewpoint. Clear treatment of physical acoustics, auditory apparatus, sound perception, development of musical skills, nature of musical feeling, host of other topics. 88 figures. 408pp. 5⅜ x 8½. 21851-1

THE PHILOSOPHY OF HISTORY, Georg W. Hegel. Great classic of Western thought develops concept that history is not chance but rational process, the evolution of freedom. 457pp. 5⅜ x 8½. 20112-0

THE BOOK OF TEA, Kakuzo Okakura. Minor classic of the Orient: entertaining, charming explanation, interpretation of traditional Japanese culture in terms of tea ceremony. 94pp. 5⅜ x 8½. 20070-1

LIFE IN ANCIENT EGYPT, Adolf Erman. Fullest, most thorough, detailed older account with much not in more recent books, domestic life, religion, magic, medicine, commerce, much more. Many illustrations reproduce tomb paintings, carvings, hieroglyphs, etc. 597pp. 5⅜ x 8½. 22632-8

SUNDIALS, Their Theory and Construction, Albert Waugh. Far and away the best, most thorough coverage of ideas, mathematics concerned, types, construction, adjusting anywhere. Simple, nontechnical treatment allows even children to build several of these dials. Over 100 illustrations. 230pp. 5⅜ x 8½. 22947-5

THEORETICAL HYDRODYNAMICS, L. M. Milne-Thomson. Classic exposition of the mathematical theory of fluid motion, applicable to both hydrodynamics and aerodynamics. Over 600 exercises. 768pp. 6⅛ x 9¼. 68970-0

SONGS OF EXPERIENCE: Facsimile Reproduction with 26 Plates in Full Color, William Blake. 26 full-color plates from a rare 1826 edition. Includes "The Tyger," "London," "Holy Thursday," and other poems. Printed text of poems. 48pp. 5¼ x 7. 24636-1

OLD-TIME VIGNETTES IN FULL COLOR, Carol Belanger Grafton (ed.). Over 390 charming, often sentimental illustrations, selected from archives of Victorian graphics–pretty women posing, children playing, food, flowers, kittens and puppies, smiling cherubs, birds and butterflies, much more. All copyright-free. 48pp. 9¼ x 12¼. 27269-9

PERSPECTIVE FOR ARTISTS, Rex Vicat Cole. Depth, perspective of sky and sea, shadows, much more, not usually covered. 391 diagrams, 81 reproductions of drawings and paintings. 279pp. 5⅜ x 8½. 22487-2

DRAWING THE LIVING FIGURE, Joseph Sheppard. Innovative approach to artistic anatomy focuses on specifics of surface anatomy, rather than muscles and bones. Over 170 drawings of live models in front, back and side views, and in widely varying poses. Accompanying diagrams. 177 illustrations. Introduction. Index. 144pp. 8⅜ x11¼. 26723-7

GOTHIC AND OLD ENGLISH ALPHABETS: 100 Complete Fonts, Dan X. Solo. Add power, elegance to posters, signs, other graphics with 100 stunning copyright-free alphabets: Blackstone, Dolbey, Germania, 97 more–including many lower-case, numerals, punctuation marks. 104pp. 8⅛ x 11. 24695-7

HOW TO DO BEADWORK, Mary White. Fundamental book on craft from simple projects to five-bead chains and woven works. 106 illustrations. 142pp. 5⅜ x 8. 20697-1

THE BOOK OF WOOD CARVING, Charles Marshall Sayers. Finest book for beginners discusses fundamentals and offers 34 designs. "Absolutely first rate . . . well thought out and well executed."–E. J. Tangerman. 118pp. 7¾ x 10⅝. 23654-4

ILLUSTRATED CATALOG OF CIVIL WAR MILITARY GOODS: Union Army Weapons, Insignia, Uniform Accessories, and Other Equipment, Schuyler, Hartley, and Graham. Rare, profusely illustrated 1846 catalog includes Union Army uniform and dress regulations, arms and ammunition, coats, insignia, flags, swords, rifles, etc. 226 illustrations. 160pp. 9 x 12. 24939-5

WOMEN'S FASHIONS OF THE EARLY 1900s: An Unabridged Republication of "New York Fashions, 1909," National Cloak & Suit Co. Rare catalog of mail-order fashions documents women's and children's clothing styles shortly after the turn of the century. Captions offer full descriptions, prices. Invaluable resource for fashion, costume historians. Approximately 725 illustrations. 128pp. 8⅜ x 11¼. 27276-1

THE 1912 AND 1915 GUSTAV STICKLEY FURNITURE CATALOGS, Gustav Stickley. With over 200 detailed illustrations and descriptions, these two catalogs are essential reading and reference materials and identification guides for Stickley furniture. Captions cite materials, dimensions and prices. 112pp. 6½ x 9¼. 26676-1

EARLY AMERICAN LOCOMOTIVES, John H. White, Jr. Finest locomotive engravings from early 19th century: historical (1804–74), main-line (after 1870), special, foreign, etc. 147 plates. 142pp. 11⅜ x 8¼. 22772-3

THE TALL SHIPS OF TODAY IN PHOTOGRAPHS, Frank O. Braynard. Lavishly illustrated tribute to nearly 100 majestic contemporary sailing vessels: Amerigo Vespucci, Clearwater, Constitution, Eagle, Mayflower, Sea Cloud, Victory, many more. Authoritative captions provide statistics, background on each ship. 190 black-and-white photographs and illustrations. Introduction. 128pp. 8⅞ x 11¾. 27163-3

LITTLE BOOK OF EARLY AMERICAN CRAFTS AND TRADES, Peter Stockham (ed.). 1807 children's book explains crafts and trades: baker, hatter, cooper, potter, and many others. 23 copperplate illustrations. 140pp. 4⅝ x 6. 23336-7

VICTORIAN FASHIONS AND COSTUMES FROM HARPER'S BAZAR, 1867–1898, Stella Blum (ed.). Day costumes, evening wear, sports clothes, shoes, hats, other accessories in over 1,000 detailed engravings. 320pp. 9⅜ x 12¼. 22990-4

GUSTAV STICKLEY, THE CRAFTSMAN, Mary Ann Smith. Superb study surveys broad scope of Stickley's achievement, especially in architecture. Design philosophy, rise and fall of the Craftsman empire, descriptions and floor plans for many Craftsman houses, more. 86 black-and-white halftones. 31 line illustrations. Introduction 208pp. 6½ x 9¼. 27210-9

THE LONG ISLAND RAIL ROAD IN EARLY PHOTOGRAPHS, Ron Ziel. Over 220 rare photos, informative text document origin (1844) and development of rail service on Long Island. Vintage views of early trains, locomotives, stations, passengers, crews, much more. Captions. 8⅞ x 11¾. 26301-0

VOYAGE OF THE LIBERDADE, Joshua Slocum. Great 19th-century mariner's thrilling, first-hand account of the wreck of his ship off South America, the 35-foot boat he built from the wreckage, and its remarkable voyage home. 128pp. 5⅜ x 8½. 40022-0

TEN BOOKS ON ARCHITECTURE, Vitruvius. The most important book ever written on architecture. Early Roman aesthetics, technology, classical orders, site selection, all other aspects. Morgan translation. 331pp. 5⅜ x 8½. 20645-9

THE HUMAN FIGURE IN MOTION, Eadweard Muybridge. More than 4,500 stopped-action photos, in action series, showing undraped men, women, children jumping, lying down, throwing, sitting, wrestling, carrying, etc. 390pp. 7⅞ x 10⅝. 20204-6 Clothbd.

TREES OF THE EASTERN AND CENTRAL UNITED STATES AND CANADA, William M. Harlow. Best one-volume guide to 140 trees. Full descriptions, woodlore, range, etc. Over 600 illustrations. Handy size. 288pp. 4½ x 6⅜. 20395-6

SONGS OF WESTERN BIRDS, Dr. Donald J. Borror. Complete song and call repertoire of 60 western species, including flycatchers, juncoes, cactus wrens, many more–includes fully illustrated booklet. Cassette and manual 99913-0

GROWING AND USING HERBS AND SPICES, Milo Miloradovich. Versatile handbook provides all the information needed for cultivation and use of all the herbs and spices available in North America. 4 illustrations. Index. Glossary. 236pp. 5⅜ x 8½. 25058-X

BIG BOOK OF MAZES AND LABYRINTHS, Walter Shepherd. 50 mazes and labyrinths in all–classical, solid, ripple, and more–in one great volume. Perfect inexpensive puzzler for clever youngsters. Full solutions. 112pp. 8⅛ x 11. 22951-3

PIANO TUNING, J. Cree Fischer. Clearest, best book for beginner, amateur. Simple repairs, raising dropped notes, tuning by easy method of flattened fifths. No previous skills needed. 4 illustrations. 201pp. 5⅜ x 8½. 23267-0

HINTS TO SINGERS, Lillian Nordica. Selecting the right teacher, developing confidence, overcoming stage fright, and many other important skills receive thoughtful discussion in this indispensible guide, written by a world-famous diva of four decades' experience. 96pp. 5⅜ x 8½. 40094-8

THE COMPLETE NONSENSE OF EDWARD LEAR, Edward Lear. All nonsense limericks, zany alphabets, Owl and Pussycat, songs, nonsense botany, etc., illustrated by Lear. Total of 320pp. 5⅜ x 8½. (Available in U.S. only.) 20167-8

VICTORIAN PARLOUR POETRY: An Annotated Anthology, Michael R. Turner. 117 gems by Longfellow, Tennyson, Browning, many lesser-known poets. "The Village Blacksmith," "Curfew Must Not Ring Tonight," "Only a Baby Small," dozens more, often difficult to find elsewhere. Index of poets, titles, first lines. xxiii + 325pp. 5⅜ x 8¼. 27044-0

DUBLINERS, James Joyce. Fifteen stories offer vivid, tightly focused observations of the lives of Dublin's poorer classes. At least one, "The Dead," is considered a masterpiece. Reprinted complete and unabridged from standard edition. 160pp. 5³⁄₁₆ x 8¼. 26870-5

GREAT WEIRD TALES: 14 Stories by Lovecraft, Blackwood, Machen and Others, S. T. Joshi (ed.). 14 spellbinding tales, including "The Sin Eater," by Fiona McLeod, "The Eye Above the Mantel," by Frank Belknap Long, as well as renowned works by R. H. Barlow, Lord Dunsany, Arthur Machen, W. C. Morrow and eight other masters of the genre. 256pp. 5⅜ x 8½. (Available in U.S. only.) 40436-6

THE BOOK OF THE SACRED MAGIC OF ABRAMELIN THE MAGE, translated by S. MacGregor Mathers. Medieval manuscript of ceremonial magic. Basic document in Aleister Crowley, Golden Dawn groups. 268pp. 5⅜ x 8½. 23211-5

NEW RUSSIAN-ENGLISH AND ENGLISH-RUSSIAN DICTIONARY, M. A. O'Brien. This is a remarkably handy Russian dictionary, containing a surprising amount of information, including over 70,000 entries. 366pp. 4½ x 6⅛. 20208-9

HISTORIC HOMES OF THE AMERICAN PRESIDENTS, Second, Revised Edition, Irvin Haas. A traveler's guide to American Presidential homes, most open to the public, depicting and describing homes occupied by every American President from George Washington to George Bush. With visiting hours, admission charges, travel routes. 175 photographs. Index. 160pp. 8¼ x 11. 26751-2

NEW YORK IN THE FORTIES, Andreas Feininger. 162 brilliant photographs by the well-known photographer, formerly with *Life* magazine. Commuters, shoppers, Times Square at night, much else from city at its peak. Captions by John von Hartz. 181pp. 9¼ x 10¾. 23585-8

INDIAN SIGN LANGUAGE, William Tomkins. Over 525 signs developed by Sioux and other tribes. Written instructions and diagrams. Also 290 pictographs. 111pp. 6⅛ x 9¼. 22029-X

THE WIT AND HUMOR OF OSCAR WILDE, Alvin Redman (ed.). More than 1,000 ripostes, paradoxes, wisecracks: Work is the curse of the drinking classes; I can resist everything except temptation; etc. 258pp. 5⅜ x 8½. 20602-5

SHAKESPEARE LEXICON AND QUOTATION DICTIONARY, Alexander Schmidt. Full definitions, locations, shades of meaning in every word in plays and poems. More than 50,000 exact quotations. 1,485pp. 6½ x 9¼. 2-vol. set.
Vol. 1: 22726-X
Vol. 2: 22727-8

SELECTED POEMS, Emily Dickinson. Over 100 best-known, best-loved poems by one of America's foremost poets, reprinted from authoritative early editions. No comparable edition at this price. Index of first lines. 64pp. 5³⁄₁₆ x 8¼. 26466-1

THE INSIDIOUS DR. FU-MANCHU, Sax Rohmer. The first of the popular mystery series introduces a pair of English detectives to their archnemesis, the diabolical Dr. Fu-Manchu. Flavorful atmosphere, fast-paced action, and colorful characters enliven this classic of the genre. 208pp. 5³⁄₁₆ x 8¼. 29898-1

THE MALLEUS MALEFICARUM OF KRAMER AND SPRENGER, translated by Montague Summers. Full text of most important witchhunter's "bible," used by both Catholics and Protestants. 278pp. 6⅝ x 10. 22802-9

SPANISH STORIES/CUENTOS ESPAÑOLES: A Dual-Language Book, Angel Flores (ed.). Unique format offers 13 great stories in Spanish by Cervantes, Borges, others. Faithful English translations on facing pages. 352pp. 5⅜ x 8½. 25399-6

GARDEN CITY, LONG ISLAND, IN EARLY PHOTOGRAPHS, 1869–1919, Mildred H. Smith. Handsome treasury of 118 vintage pictures, accompanied by carefully researched captions, document the Garden City Hotel fire (1899), the Vanderbilt Cup Race (1908), the first airmail flight departing from the Nassau Boulevard Aerodrome (1911), and much more. 96pp. 8⅞ x 11¾. 40669-5

OLD QUEENS, N.Y., IN EARLY PHOTOGRAPHS, Vincent F. Seyfried and William Asadorian. Over 160 rare photographs of Maspeth, Jamaica, Jackson Heights, and other areas. Vintage views of DeWitt Clinton mansion, 1939 World's Fair and more. Captions. 192pp. 8⅞ x 11. 26358-4

CAPTURED BY THE INDIANS: 15 Firsthand Accounts, 1750-1870, Frederick Drimmer. Astounding true historical accounts of grisly torture, bloody conflicts, relentless pursuits, miraculous escapes and more, by people who lived to tell the tale. 384pp. 5⅜ x 8½. 24901-8

THE WORLD'S GREAT SPEECHES (Fourth Enlarged Edition), Lewis Copeland, Lawrence W. Lamm, and Stephen J. McKenna. Nearly 300 speeches provide public speakers with a wealth of updated quotes and inspiration–from Pericles' funeral oration and William Jennings Bryan's "Cross of Gold Speech" to Malcolm X's powerful words on the Black Revolution and Earl of Spenser's tribute to his sister, Diana, Princess of Wales. 944pp. 5⅜ x 8⅜. 40903-1

THE BOOK OF THE SWORD, Sir Richard F. Burton. Great Victorian scholar/adventurer's eloquent, erudite history of the "queen of weapons"–from prehistory to early Roman Empire. Evolution and development of early swords, variations (sabre, broadsword, cutlass, scimitar, etc.), much more. 336pp. 6⅛ x 9¼.
25434-8

AUTOBIOGRAPHY: The Story of My Experiments with Truth, Mohandas K. Gandhi. Boyhood, legal studies, purification, the growth of the Satyagraha (nonviolent protest) movement. Critical, inspiring work of the man responsible for the freedom of India. 480pp. 5⅜ x 8½. (Available in U.S. only.) 24593-4

CELTIC MYTHS AND LEGENDS, T. W. Rolleston. Masterful retelling of Irish and Welsh stories and tales. Cuchulain, King Arthur, Deirdre, the Grail, many more. First paperback edition. 58 full-page illustrations. 512pp. 5⅜ x 8½. 26507-2

THE PRINCIPLES OF PSYCHOLOGY, William James. Famous long course complete, unabridged. Stream of thought, time perception, memory, experimental methods; great work decades ahead of its time. 94 figures. 1,391pp. 5⅜ x 8½. 2-vol. set.
Vol. I: 20381-6 Vol. II: 20382-4

THE WORLD AS WILL AND REPRESENTATION, Arthur Schopenhauer. Definitive English translation of Schopenhauer's life work, correcting more than 1,000 errors, omissions in earlier translations. Translated by E. F. J. Payne. Total of 1,269pp. 5⅜ x 8½. 2-vol. set. Vol. 1: 21761-2 Vol. 2: 21762-0

MAGIC AND MYSTERY IN TIBET, Madame Alexandra David-Neel. Experiences among lamas, magicians, sages, sorcerers, Bonpa wizards. A true psychic discovery. 32 illustrations. 321pp. 5⅜ x 8½. (Available in U.S. only.) 22682-4

THE EGYPTIAN BOOK OF THE DEAD, E. A. Wallis Budge. Complete reproduction of Ani's papyrus, finest ever found. Full hieroglyphic text, interlinear transliteration, word-for-word translation, smooth translation. 533pp. 6½ x 9¼. 21866-X

MATHEMATICS FOR THE NONMATHEMATICIAN, Morris Kline. Detailed, college-level treatment of mathematics in cultural and historical context, with numerous exercises. Recommended Reading Lists. Tables. Numerous figures. 641pp. 5⅜ x 8½.
24823-2

PROBABILISTIC METHODS IN THE THEORY OF STRUCTURES, Isaac Elishakoff. Well-written introduction covers the elements of the theory of probability from two or more random variables, the reliability of such multivariable structures, the theory of random function, Monte Carlo methods of treating problems incapable of exact solution, and more. Examples. 502pp. 5⅜ x 8½. 40691-1

THE RIME OF THE ANCIENT MARINER, Gustave Doré, S. T. Coleridge. Doré's finest work; 34 plates capture moods, subtleties of poem. Flawless full-size reproductions printed on facing pages with authoritative text of poem. "Beautiful. Simply beautiful."–*Publisher's Weekly*. 77pp. 9¼ x 12. 22305-1

NORTH AMERICAN INDIAN DESIGNS FOR ARTISTS AND CRAFTSPEOPLE, Eva Wilson. Over 360 authentic copyright-free designs adapted from Navajo blankets, Hopi pottery, Sioux buffalo hides, more. Geometrics, symbolic figures, plant and animal motifs, etc. 128pp. 8⅜ x 11. (Not for sale in the United Kingdom.) 25341-4

SCULPTURE: Principles and Practice, Louis Slobodkin. Step-by-step approach to clay, plaster, metals, stone; classical and modern. 253 drawings, photos. 255pp. 8⅛ x 11.
22960-2

THE INFLUENCE OF SEA POWER UPON HISTORY, 1660–1783, A. T. Mahan. Influential classic of naval history and tactics still used as text in war colleges. First paperback edition. 4 maps. 24 battle plans. 640pp. 5⅜ x 8½. 25509-3